Waiting for the End of the World

Marina

"In a week and a half it won't matter," I said.

"If he's right," the boy added, "it won't."

"Or if he's wrong," I said, like a traitor. It was a wonder lightning didn't strike the ground between us. I waited another second, then got up, wiped my hands on my jeans, and walked back down the hill.

I still didn't know the boy's name, but I knew something more important. It was less than two weeks till the end of the world, less than two weeks till my fourteenth birthday, and I had just fallen in love for the first time in my life.

My timing sure was awful.

Jed

You know how it is: as soon as you decide to forget something, your brain comes to the conclusion that it's the most fascinating thing in the world.

So I spent most of the afternoon thinking about the girl.

Or, to use Believer talk, The Girl.

And her Chestnut Hair.

The thing I want to know is, if you tell your brain not to do stuff like that and it keeps doing it anyway, does that mean your mind has a mind of its own? And if it does, then who's in charge here, anyway?

It's a wonder we're not *all* lunatics.

Jane Yolen & Bruce Coville

Armageddon Summer

SCHOLASTIC INC.

New York   Toronto   London   Auckland   Sydney
Mexico City   New Delhi   Hong Kong

ISBN 0-439-16556-3

Published by Scholastic Inc., 555 Broadway, New York, NY 10012, by arrangement with Harcourt Brace & Company.

12 11 10 9 8 7 6 5 4 3 2 1   0 1 2 3 4 5/0

Printed in the U.S.A.   01

First Scholastic printing, March 2000

Text set in Perpetua

Designed by Camilla Filancia

For MARY *and* WINI,

in memory of

our Centrum days

Marina

It all began at dinner one night last fall, when Mom announced, right after grace, "I've had a revelation."

It was so astonishing no one moved, not even to pass the macaroni and cheese. We just sat there waiting to hear the rest.

"I'm going to teach the children at home," Mom said.

"Myrna," Dad told her, "that revelation only reveals you're tired of cleaning houses."

"It's true that cleaning someone else's slop is awful," she said, "when I've got so much of my own at home. But that's not the true reason. The true reason is that Reverend Beelson says the schools are corrupting our children and those who are corrupted will burn in the fires of Hell."

Well, that started our own little version of Hell. Mom and Dad began to snipe at each other like soldiers on a personal battlefield, the worst fight ever. It was so awful Leo started to cry. I grabbed him up and took him out onto the porch rocker. I sang him lullabies—"All the Pretty Little Horses" and "Dance to Your Daddy" and "Rock-a-Bye, Baby"—all of which he still loved, though he was way past three.

But the older boys stayed through the whole thing, reporting out to me on the porch now and again like war correspondents on CNN.

Dad was wrong about Mom's revelation. It had nothing to do with house cleaning. It had to do with heart cleaning. Mom had become a Believer.

She'd been one for some time, of course, only with a small *b*. We were all good Christians in a general way—even Dad, though he always *bah-humbug*ged his way through Christmas. Being a Christian was like having brown eyes or dark hair. We never actually thought about it. We just *were*. But none of the churches we visited had ever taken us over before. Or taken us on.

Not until Reverend Beelson's Church of the Believers, that is.

We were welcomed there. We were made part of a greater family of worshipers—instead of just some crazy bunch of religion gypsies who dropped in one Sunday and were gone the next, which is how Dad once described us.

Home schooling may have been Reverend Beelson's idea, but Mom took to it with the conviction of a convert. It took her just a week of lobbying till Dad finally agreed to let her teach us at home. I think Mom just wore him down. "She's a regular little whetstone," Dad sometimes said.

"But," he told her, "if you're going to stop working for money and start working for God, I'll have to work all the harder for the family."

She nodded. It was an old fight between them.

"After all," he added, "God don't bother His head about new shoes or dentists. And Marina's getting on to

2

fourteen and is going to need a whole bunch of new clothes."

I remember that argument as if it happened yesterday. I had just put Leo and the other boys to bed—always my job—and was going to bed myself, when I heard the *squeak-squawk* of the rocking chair in the living room. It brought me creeping down the stairs to sit on the bottom step and listen. I wasn't usually into eavesdropping, but with things so tense all the time, it was almost a kind of duty. I had to know what was going on. To be prepared, you see.

Mom and Dad were already well into the fight when I got there, because Mom's chair was going back and forth pretty fast, a sure sign she was angry. Dad said something about our paying for the doctor, and Mom's chair stopped rocking.

That was a bad sign. The chair getting quiet. Mom getting quiet.

"What about the children, Harmon?" she asked in something close to a whisper, though I could hear every word. "Don't you care about them, more than doctors and dentists and new clothes? Don't you care about their souls?"

"Souls is women's work, Myrn. If you want them kids to be Believers, they will be."

"They already are," she said. "No thanks to you."

"That they are *at all*," he said, his voice getting dangerously quiet, "is thanks to me. You'd have gotten rid of Marina before she was ever born, if you remember. It was me wanted to keep her. Me wanted to get married. It was *me* made this family."

"And it's you breaking it up now," she said.

The argument made my stomach become a stone. Big and hard and cold. I don't think I could have moved back up the stairs and away from it even if I'd wanted to. My body was still but my mind was racing around like a runner who'd lost the track.

Until that minute, you see, I had gone along with Mom to each new church every Sunday, and they'd all seemed about the same: same songs, same prayers, same sermons. God had seemed the same, too: a distant, not-unkind grandfather up in the sky.

But suddenly I had a revelation of my own. It was about us—about the family, about staying together through whatever else might happen. And I also saw that it was important for Mom to be right about Reverend Beelson and about the Believers and God. Our entire family depended upon it.

So I prayed, *Let me Believe, God. Let me Believe everything.*

Because, I thought, if I believed, then Mom would be right. And in a way Dad would be right, too. And if they were both right together, then the family would be all right as well.

"Everything," I said out loud, to be sure God heard.

And He must have, because that was the exact moment that I became a Believer.

2

Jed

I would have missed the end of the world if my mother hadn't taken off with that photographer from Colorado. But she did, which meant that Dad went a little crazy for a while.

The crazy part I could understand. Heck, I acted a little weird myself for the first month or so. But even if you're not entirely happy with your family (and who is?) you still expect it to stay in one piece. And you sure don't expect your own personal mother to go off on some wild romantic fling—especially if that mother is something as normal and boring as a high school science teacher.

My version of crazy mostly showed up in school, where I started getting in real trouble. You could have summed up all the teacher comments I got in the last quarter of the year with the words, *Jed has an attitude problem.*

Five words, and they think they've said everything there is to say about you.

Dad's version of crazy showed up at home, where he stopped doing much of anything at all, except moping around.

5

Well, moping around and drinking.

Personally, I think it would have been better if he had let it all out——you know, punched a few holes in the wall or busted up some furniture or something. But after two months of moping and sighing, what did he do?

He went out and got religion!

I don't mean he suddenly changed from an atheist to a godboy. Our family had always been churchgoers, Mom, Dad, my big sister, Alice (who was lucky enough to leave for college before all this started), and I trooping off to First Methodist every Sunday morning like a perfect flock of little lambs. I didn't mind church all that much, though when I got older I used to fight with Mom and Dad about having to go. But that was mostly for the sake of making a fuss. I had a lot of friends there, and we usually had a fairly good time.

But after Mom took off, Dad stopped going to our old church. I think he was embarrassed. Wild flings weren't supposed to happen in a Methodist family. Congregationalist, maybe. But not in our church.

Reverend Hill came by to talk three or four times, but after the first time Dad didn't want to see him and pretended not to be home. This meant that I got to lie to Reverend Hill ("No, sir, I don't expect Dad back for several hours yet"), which was a new and fairly uncomfortable experience.

Given all that, I was kind of surprised when Dad went out and found a new church. That was when he got religion in a big way. I thought the Methodists took God pretty seriously, they were nothing compared to Reverend Raymond Beelson's Believers. Once Dad joined the flock (as he called it) things changed around our house, and fast.

Of course, it was just Dad and me by then, my mother having answered the call of the wild with her studly photographer, and Alice being off at her college's summer program.

The first noticeable change was that Dad stopped drinking. That was fine as far as I was concerned. He wasn't a mean drunk, like Howard's dad, or a disappearing drunk, like John's, who sometimes took off for three or four days at a time when he was on a toot.

No, my father was a weeper.

It was pretty embarrassing. Disgusting, actually. It's hard to look up to your father after you've seen him drunk and blubbering.

It made me mad.

To be fair, that only happened once—the third night after Mom left, to be precise. After he finally went to sleep I rounded up all the booze in the house. Then I carried it into the kitchen and poured it down the sink. I took real pleasure in watching it disappear, even though I figured there'd be hell to pay when Dad figured out what I had done.

I was wrong about that; he didn't say a thing, just looked kind of sad and sheepish. But I guess he wasn't all that sheepish, since two days later he had replaced every bottle.

The drinking ended the day someone dragged Dad to a meeting at Reverend Raymond Beelson's Church of the Believers. I might actually have been grateful for the change, except it wasn't just the booze that went—it was the coffee and the television set, too. Then we started having fights about my hair. For a day or so I was afraid he was even going to try to make me get rid of my laptop—which would have meant a real battle, let me tell you. Fortunately he didn't do more than make a few vague mutterings about that.

And then we had our little chat about Armageddon.

It was not a pretty conversation. But then that was true of most of the talks we had had since Dad joined the Believers.

It started after dinner one night in early July. I was clearing the table (it had been his turn to cook) when he said, "Jed, please come into the living room when you're done. I have something serious to discuss with you."

What have I done now? I wondered.

Once we were sitting, I noticed that Dad looked uncomfortable. He glanced from side to side, down at his hands, anywhere but directly at my face. Finally he took a deep breath, looked right at me, and said, "I don't know any easy way to tell you this, son, but Reverend Beelson has had a revelation."

I sat, waiting for him to continue. After a long silence, I said, "And . . .?"

Staring directly into my eyes, Dad said, "On July twenty-seventh the world as we know it is going to end."

3

Marina

Dad began working two shifts at the plant every day instead of occasionally—five A.M. to one P.M., and then two till ten. He said it was his only way to keep the family together, but somehow it didn't feel like that at all. We hardly saw him anymore. By the time he came home from work, only Grahame and I were still up, and Dad was too tired to talk much anyway. It meant the house was quieter, of course, since Mom and Dad were never in the same place long enough to fight. But if that was a blessing, why did it feel like a curse?

Mom taught us in the living room, at different stations. Being the only girl and the oldest, I got the dinner table. Grahame, who's four years younger than me but is the oldest boy, got Grandy's rolltop desk. Martin and the twins had to work on their laps. Leo was, of course, too little yet for anything much except the ABCs and numbers and coloring. We all took turns reading him stories. His favorite was "The Elephant's Child."

We had math and spelling, geography, history, and English, just like in real school. I had gone there through seventh grade, so I knew what was what.

Mom could handle all those subjects easily. She'd been an A student once, though she quit high school to have me. And she was a great reader, mostly of the Bible, or books about history or prayer or 1,001 ways to make things out of leftovers. But science was a problem, since Mom didn't care much for it.

She once said to me, "Science is how men explain God's works to each other. But as for me, I don't need to know about eternal combustion to drive into Heaven." She didn't need to know about it to drive into Springfield, either. But I understood what she meant. She has a natural gift for metaphor, which comes from reading the Bible so much. I have it, too. Sometimes I wish we all spoke the way God speaks in the Testaments. The world would be better off for it.

But Mom's hating science was especially hard on Grahame, who is naturally curious, like the elephant's child. He complained about it all the time, until finally Mom took to buying him books about science from the Olde Bookstore in Northampton. He ate them up, spitting out what he read in little sound bites at dinner.

"Did you know..." his sentences all began. And they ended with things like "Beluga neckbones aren't fused together like other whales'." Or "Some dinosaurs were the size of pigeons." In that way we all learned something about science, though it was *Jeopardy!* science according to Dad.

You might think that staying home meant we had no friends, and I guess I was the one who'd been especially worried about that. I had been best friends with Sonia and Amity since first grade. We'd even made a pact at the end of elementary school that we would stay close in junior high, no matter what, spitting in our palms and shaking hands on it.

However, the odd thing about home schooling was that instead of having no friends, what happened was just the opposite. We had lots of them. We got to do activities with other home schoolers, like go to the Basketball Hall of Fame or the Yankee Candle Company or the Emily Dickinson Homestead in Amherst—she's my absolute favorite poet.

I also got to be pen pals on the Internet with kids from as far away as Japan because Mom found out there was a special Home School Listserv. We weren't allowed to surf the Net, of course, though sometimes Grahame did it when Mom was off grocery shopping.

So with all the home-school outings and the Internet as well, I actually didn't have any time to miss Amity or Sonia at all. Not even a little.

Of course, being a Believer meant more than just home schooling. It meant there wasn't any beer allowed in the house, or anything with caffeine in it, or any smoking. We kids didn't smoke or drink beer, of course, but Dad did. You'd be surprised at what has caffeine in it, though—Pepsi and Coke. And chocolate.

Chocolate was the hardest to give up. I love chocolate.

No TV was another of Reverend Beelson's rules. That was especially difficult for Grahame, who had watched *Nova* the way Mom watched Reverend Beelson at church. Religiously. Dad would turn on the TV the moment he got home, so if we were still awake, the temptation to watch it with him was great. Especially if it meant sitting next to

11

him on the sofa, snugged up close. Mom said that since Dad wasn't yet a Believer, she couldn't very well ask him to get rid of the TV. "Besides," she reminded us, "resisting temptation is good for the soul."

Reverend Beelson didn't say anything specifically in his sermons about the Internet. So Mom let us continue with any pen pals who were religious, though that word covered a lot. For example, Yoko, in Japan, was a Buddhist. I didn't tell Mom that.

And I tried not to mind too much about all the things I had to give up. After all, I had asked God for belief and got it. Big time.

So when Reverend Beelson proclaimed Armageddon that Sunday morning in June, thundering down at us the actual date for the end of the world from his pulpit, none of us Believers were particularly surprised.

The Bible says that there is going to be hail and fire mingled with blood and that a third part of the earth will be burnt up and a third part of the sea become blood and a third part of the stars will be darkened, and stuff like that.

And with the ebola virus and serial killers and Middle East terrorists and floods all over the Midwest, with earthquakes in L.A. and global warming changing our weather, with planes dropping out of the sky and the tornado that ran through the town next to ours picking up a car with a teacher and three students—it did look pretty much like the world was about to end. Even Grahame could see that scientifically.

So we believed.

"July twenty-seventh!" Reverend Beelson roared. "The fire burning and the seas overflowing and the wicked drowning in their own blood. But we Believers will be on a mountaintop, and so we will be saved."

He wasn't just talking pretty when he said "a mountaintop." He wasn't even making what my favorite teacher, Ms. Leatherby, used to jokingly call a meddlefur. He meant a real mountaintop, with big tall pine trees, a dirt road spiraling up the side, and a wind-chill factor about equal to the Yukon's, even in summer.

He meant Mount Weeupcut.

Only, not being from around here but from Boston, he didn't say it correctly. He pronounced the *p*.

Grahame elbowed me and whispered, "Wee-a-cut," which is of course the right way to say it but the wrong thing to comment on in church. Mom shushed him and gave him the Look. No one who has ever been given the Look thinks twice about disobeying.

"July twenty-seventh," Reverend Beelson repeated, "in this year of our Lord two thousand, is the Day of Atonement. It is the Day of Anointment. It is the Day of Armageddon."

And the Day of Alliteration, I thought. *Plus capital letters*. I may not have said it aloud, like Grahame would, but it was just as much a blasphemy. And an unkindness to Reverend Beelson, who was working so hard to save us.

"It is the day that the Believers alone, Angels on the mountaintop, will start the world afresh," Reverend Beelson said.

All around me, grown-up voices called out, "Amen!" as if the word was a hall pass into Heaven. We children, being new at redemption though old hands at sinning, added our own voices just a beat or two behind.

"Amen!" Grahame shouted.

13

"Amen," Martin sang out.

"Amen," I whispered.

I wasn't too embarrassed to shout. And it wasn't that I didn't believe enough to say it out loud. I had promised God to believe and I was keeping my promise. It was just that God could hear me whether I shouted or whispered.

Besides, there was this awful nagging feeling inside me that God already knew I wasn't entirely sure I wanted to be saved. Not on a mountaintop and not without my dad, who would probably be well into overtime pay on July 27, it being a Thursday.

I knew it would be a Thursday because July 27, 2000, was not only the Day of Atonement, the Day of Anointment, the Day of Armageddon, the Day of Alliteration...

It was my fourteenth birthday as well.

4

Jed

When my father told me that the world was going to end I figured he was making some sort of weird joke. I made a *yeah-right* kind of snort. But he just shook his head slightly, and suddenly I could tell that he was serious.

"Dad!"

He closed his eyes. "I know, I know. It sounds a little strange. But believe me, Jeddie"—I *hate* being called Jeddie—"I've looked at this very carefully. Reverend Beelson is a serious scholar. He's studied the Scriptures, done the calculations over and over. There's really no room for doubt. The signs are clear. The last days are upon us."

I was too shocked to make a wisecrack about Reverend Beelson having bad math skills. My own dad, a little moody, occasionally drunk, but not that bad a guy overall, had just lost his mind.

What made it even worse was that he didn't *look* cuckoo. He just looked like Dad. Same graying sandy hair just starting to thin, same big nose, same bristling mustache. Only the eyes were different. For a long time they had been set on perma-sad, as if he was just a minute away from bursting into tears. Now they were bright and clear, excited and happy. The way they used to be before Mom left. Actually, a long time before Mom left, now that I thought about it.

It was so good to see him that way again that I had a weird moment when I wondered if what he said might possibly be true, and the world *was* going to end on July 27.

I forced myself back to the real world. "Dad, everyone knows Beelson is a nutcase! You should hear the things they say about him in school."

My father looked at me sadly. "I thought you didn't believe in basing your life on what everyone else says, Mr. Nonconformist."

"OK, skip what everyone else says. *I* think he's nuts."

Dad's voice got sharp. "Raymond Beelson is a great man. Not only that, he's the man who's going to save our lives. Alice's, too, if I can get her here. Obviously I cannot *force* you to believe that. Fortunately for you, the Lord is merciful, and will make exceptions for those who are still young."

I thought about pointing out that if the Lord was really merciful, He would also make exceptions for the billions of kids whose parents didn't belong to Beelson's nutty congregation. But I decided not to press the point.

Dad put his hands together and stared straight into my eyes. "On July twenty-seventh, which will be more terrible than any day has ever been, you and I will be safe on the top of Mount Weeupcut with the rest of the Believers. It's a miracle for us, Jed. But it's going to be a great responsibility, too. We will be the beginning of the world to come, the first children of the New Era. It will be our job to pick up the pieces of the world that used to be, and make from them a new paradise."

At the moment all I wanted to pick up were the pieces of my father's brain, which seemed to have fallen out of his head.

"Just out of curiosity—when do we leave for this little trip to Wonderland?"

"Jed!"

"Sorry. Dad."

Notice I didn't say *what* I was sorry for. But then that list would have been too long to cover in one conversation, since it included, for starters:

1. I was sorry my mother had left;
2. I was even sorrier I didn't know where she was, so I could go live with her;
3. I was sorrier still that my father had lost his mind; and
4. I was sorriest of all that I was getting roped into this nutball stuff.

I was also sorry that one small corner of my mind was already doubting my doubt, twitching with the tantalizing fear that Beelson's weird vision of the end of the world might really be true. I shook my head as if trying to drive the thought away. Just because my father had lost his mind didn't mean I had to go nuts, too. In fact it was all the more reason for me to keep my wits about me.

Dad handed me a sheet of paper. "Here's a list of things you'll need. I want you to start preparing."

"When are we going to leave?" I asked again.

"Next Saturday."

"Saturday! But July twenty-seventh is almost three weeks away!"

Dad smiled peacefully. "There will be many Believers. One hundred and forty-four, to be precise. We must go to Mount Weeupcut to prepare a place for them." He paused, then added, "The Lord will smile brightest on those who come first."

Later that night I called Alice.

"He's overreacting to Mom's leaving," she said, when I was only a few sentences into my story. She had just finished her second year as a psych major, so she was big on secret motives. "Just hold on, Jed. Daddy needs you now."

"Easy for you to say. You don't have to live with him."

"Have you talked to anyone about it? Anyone there, I mean?"

"Are you kidding? Do you think I want to get laughed out of school?"

She sighed. "You really shouldn't hold stuff in so much, Jed. It's not good for you."

"Thus sayeth the shrink-to-be."

"Thus sayeth your big sister, who knows you've done that all your life. Now listen. Dad's going through a rough patch, but I bet he'll be back to normal in a few months."

"That shows what you know. We don't *have* a few months."

"What do you mean?" asked Alice, sounding worried for the first time.

"According to Dad, the world is going to end three weeks from tomorrow. Reverend Beelson told him so."

I enjoyed telling her that more than I should have. But

18

I was tired of her being such a know-it-all ... and tired of having to deal with Dad on my own.

"Jed, are you serious?"

"Dead serious. So to speak. I expect Dad will be calling you about it himself before long. He doesn't care if Mom burns, but he definitely wants you to come to the mountaintop with us."

"What mountaintop?" asked Alice uneasily.

"The one he's going to drag me to so we don't get fried when the rest of the world turns to toast. Be sure to say you'll come when he asks, big sister. It's going to be ever so much fun. I'd hate to have you miss it."

"Oh, geez," muttered Alice. "This is worse than I thought."

"That's what I've been trying to tell you! What am I going to do?"

"Well, you'll have to go with him."

"*What?*"

"Someone's got to look out for him, Jed. I'd come myself, but I can't walk out in the middle of summer school. Besides, it will only be for a couple of weeks. Think of it as ... camping. When it's all over, things will get back to normal."

Which shows what she knew.

"Beelsonite Believers"
Obtained via Freedom of Information Act

BACKGROUND

Though the Massachusetts-based Beelsonite Believers
are a typical millennialist sect, they do have a few significant differences from other such groups. Primary
among these is their insistence that they know the precise day on which the world will end ("We know the
day, but not the hour" is a favorite phrase of theirs).
Also significant is their certainty that only a very small
number of people will be saved when this Armageddon
arrives—144 exactly, as compared to the more generous 144,000 postulated by some groups. Note the mystical aspect of the number: a dozen dozen.

Their leader, the Reverend Raymond Beelson, is a
charismatic figure with a somewhat checkered past. He
has been a professor of religion, a used-car salesman,
and a registered nurse(!). The most interesting, and
troubling, aspect of Beelson's history is the fact that
we have no record at all for three years of his life. Indeed, he seems to have vanished from the face of the
earth during that time. It was only after he resurfaced

in Boston that he began referring to himself as "Reverend" Beelson.

Beelson has had two sons, Charles (living) and Everett
(deceased). His wife, Lucille, died in 1993.

SUMMARY
The Beelsonite movement seems benign, if somewhat
eccentric. There are only two small congregations, one
in Boston, with about 150 members, and a smaller one
in western Mass., numbering about 50. While children
are not a primary concern of the group, other than in
the saving of their souls, their children do seem basically happy and well cared for. There is no indication
of any molestation, and this is certainly not a Branch
Davidian–type group.

Like many millennialist/survivalist groups, the Beel-
sonites have a fairly large stockpile of weapons. However, in this case the weapons are all legally registered,
and there are no grounds for any action in seizing
them.

RECOMMENDATION
Maintain a hands-off stance, but keep under close
watch. Leave current agent in place.

in Fresco that he wasn't referring to himself as "Everett" Beeson.

Beeson has natural sons Cadillac (Yuma) and Everett (Deceased). His wife, Lucille, died in 1993.

The Beehollac movement seems healthy. Somewhat successful are only two small congregations, one in Boston with about 150 members, and another one in western Mass. numbering about seventy.

FIRST DRAFT OF A LETTER

July 11

Dear Harmon:

 I stood by you all these years and believe me it hasn't been easy. You have a rough mouth and your a tom cat right enough. But you love your kids, I'll give you that. And your a hard worker. We never been without.

 But there's a hole inside me. I want to believe in something. Something bigger than me.

 Once it was you I believed in. That's a long time gone. And now I know you were too small to fill that hole anyway. The first time I heard about Reverend Beelson and the Believers, on that flier down at the Three County Fair, announcing a prayer meeting, I knew it was what I

22

was looking for. He tells the truth, Harmon, something you gave up on years ago.

I'm not faulting you. Your just a man. But even you could be saved if youd just come with us up on the mountain. The kids and me. We could be a family again, into the Hereafter. Its promised to us. All you have to say is yes.

Your wife, Myrna

5

Marina

The preparations took us a while. Dad was not home for any of them, which was the worst part, because we didn't just have to buy camping stuff for the month we were to be up on the mountain, we were also supposed to make our formal farewells.

The Reverend Beelson had told us how to do it, leaning over the pulpit with a sorrowful face and a soft voice. Somehow that was scarier than when he thundered at us.

"No apologies," he said. "No exhortations. And especially no appeals. Those who would know the Lord will come."

Which is all very well if your whole family is already there.

So we wrote to Grandy and Grandma Betty, notes that Mom dictated, though we were each allowed to add something personal. I told them I loved them and especially remembered the week we'd spent in Colonial Williamsburg, a week in the time before religion and the End of the World. I didn't say it quite that way, but that was what I meant.

Pop and Maymom got the same kind of postscript from

me, except for the part about Williamsburg. I thanked them for taking me to the musical plays at the university. And I told them I'd always remember how we sang Christmas carols in front of their fireplace. *Always*. That word takes on a special meaning if you are talking about eternity.

What I didn't say to them, what I couldn't, was that because the End of the World and my birthday were coinciding, I felt I was—somehow—responsible.

How?

I felt that if I had been better, or nicer, or smarter—or maybe older—all this wouldn't be happening. As Emily Dickinson says, "The Opening and the Close of Being, are alike..." I have a book with all her poems that Maymom gave me, and often I just let the pages fall open to one of them. And would you believe it—Emily always seems to know just what I am feeling.

I sent messages to my Internet pals as well, not telling them exactly what was about to happen, only that I was canceling my account because we were in the middle of a move. Mom helped me with that letter, too, because I had to be very careful how I worded it. Reverend Beelson had said that there'd be a panic if we let Unbelievers know too soon what was going to happen.

After all, Mount Weeupcut is only so big. And we were supposed to have only 144 Believers up there at the End of the World. One hundred and forty-four. No more, no less. The number came from Scriptures, so it had to be right.

But beginning the End of the World with a bunch of half lies seemed...unreligious somehow. Or un-Christian. Or just plain wrong.

However, I was the only one who seemed bothered by

this. When I brought it up at Bible study class, I was told that Believers could do no wrong and that when we spoke even a half lie, it became truth in our mouths. And besides, the man who was running the class said Reverend Beelson had told us to do it.

At home, Mom said the same.

Grahame only shrugged when I asked him what he thought, adding, "Did you know that great apes and humans are the only animals who can lie?" A Grahame kind of answer that didn't help me at all.

Because the question was not just about what lies we told but about who we were telling them to. Our grandparents and our uncles and aunts, our cousins, our teachers, our friends.

Mom drove us down to the plant to see Dad and to let him know that if and when he returned home, there wasn't going to be any home to return to. She explained it to us in the car. I think that was when I finally understood what the End of the World was about. I felt the way I always do when a fever is starting, hot and cold at once, with a strange buzzing in my ears and an ache at the base of my neck.

The funny thing was, the plant had been closed down by a strike and Dad had never even mentioned it. I think that was when I really knew we weren't a family anymore.

We found Dad on a picket line, wearing a sign on his chest that said PUT AN END TO UNFAIR PRACTICES. He was drinking a cup of steaming coffee and talking excitedly to a tall, chesty woman with improbably red hair who seemed to be standing awfully close to him. When he saw us his face got as red as her hair and he looked slightly uncomfortable, but he didn't move away from her or stop drinking, just waved as if we were some old friends coming for an unexpected visit. I wanted to shake the redheaded woman. And I wanted to grab Dad and hold him. I did neither.

"God is putting an end to all unfair practices, Harmon," Mom said without any more of a greeting. She pointed to his sign as she spoke.

He looked at her over the rim of his Styrofoam cup. "I wish it was that easy, Myrn. Honest, I do." Then he smiled at us. "Hi, kids." His voice, at least, had not changed.

"You always do things the hard way," she answered, and gave the redheaded woman the Look.

The redhead didn't respond to the Look except to laugh. She had too many teeth.

I was stunned. I had never known the Look to fail before. At the edges of my eyes I could feel tears gathering, and I prayed they would not fall. I wondered suddenly if God cared about our family. And if He did, how could He let Dad remain here when the rest of us were going to the mountain to be saved?

Do something, I prayed. Reverend Beelson had said, "No appeals," but surely he'd meant we weren't to appeal to people. I didn't think that ban applied to God.

Do anything, I prayed. But either God's time is slower than ours, or He takes a longer view.

"You know this is crazy stuff, Myrn," Dad said. "And if I didn't think a two-week camping trip would knock some sense into you, I'd be a lot more worried than I am."

"It's not camping, Harmon. It's the End of the World," Mom said.

"The end of our little part of it, anyway," he mumbled.

"You ended that part a long time ago," she answered

27

back, nodding at the redheaded woman. Then she smiled when Dad had the grace to look embarrassed.

"Myrna..." he said.

"Fry," she said.

I think I made a noise then, somewhere between a sob and a gasp, but he only laughed. The laugh made Mom turn on her heel and walk away. Her look as she passed me was what Emily Dickinson would have called *transcendent*.

The boys shook Dad's hand, all but Leo, who is young enough still for hugs. I hung around until everyone else went back to the car. Then I put my arms around Dad, partly because I needed to and partly because I wanted to remind God that we were a family here, and that families needed saving, too, whether they were all together on a mountaintop or not.

"I don't want the world to end without you, Dadda," I said, calling him by my old special name, which I suppose was just on the edge of being an appeal. His body felt warm and a little squishy, and he smelled so familiar it made my eyes finally brim over.

He didn't put down his coffee cup. But he kissed me on the top of my head, and then on my eyes, where the tears must have tasted salty. His beard and mustache tickled. Not the kind of tickling that makes you laugh but the kind that makes you feel terribly sad.

"I love you, too, baby," he said. "And when the world is over, I'll come back. For you and the boys."

Which didn't make a lot of sense at the time.

I left then and found the car. Ignoring Mom's Look and the boys' chattering, I got in. Then I made my mind a careful blank——no thoughts, no memories, no appeals.

And no more prayers, either.

Harmon—

I have taken the kids. We have gone up on the

mountain. You can decide if you want to be

afraid or fried. Don't come if you don't come

alone.

Myrna

6

Jed

In fifth grade I broke my arm by jumping out of a tree during a game of hide-and-seek. I can still hear the sound of that bone snapping. God, did it hurt. Hurt some when I broke it, but even more over the next few days, as the healing began.

It felt as if I wore that cast forever.

What I learned from that experience is that there are some things you just have to live through. Other things that have fallen into this category in my life include:

* seventh grade (a truly horrible year for me)
* any meal featuring broccoli, canned salmon, or a casserole made with cream-of-celery soup
* the month after my mother left
* the upcoming end of the world

I worked on this list as we drove to the top of Mount Weeupcut. I always make lists when I'm trying to sort my way through a problem. It's a habit I picked up from my mother.

I'm probably not the only one who learned that from Mom, since it was a tactic she taught all her students. But I suspect I got it drilled into my head more thoroughly than her students, since she had seven days a week for sixteen years to work on me.

I wondered if she thought she had taught me everything I needed to know, and therefore I didn't need her anymore. Then I forced the question, and all other thoughts of her, out of my head altogether—something I was able to do for five or ten minutes at a time on good days.

I turned to the issue of surviving this trip. The best I could tell myself was that it was only going to take a couple of weeks, and then the whole thing would be over. True, they would be weeks spent on top of a mountain, surrounded by a bunch of lunatics who thought God was going to fry the planet. But even so, there was a definite endpoint in sight.

The way I looked at it, there were three possibilities for how this little camping trip might play out:

POSSIBILITY NUMBER 1: Nothing would happen, in which case the Believers would be disappointed, but I could just go back to my life and add this to the list of things I had survived—maybe even have a good laugh about it with my friends.

POSSIBILITY NUMBER 2: The world actually would come to an end but would take all of us with it when it went. This seemed somewhat more likely than God roasting the entire planet but making it a point to spare Beelson and his lunatic followers.

POSSIBILITY NUMBER 3: Reverend Beelson was right. The world really was going to end, but those of us on the mountain would live through it.

Number 3 struck me as not only the least likely but the most horrifying. The idea of two weeks with these people, I could survive. The idea of spending the rest of my life in a world populated by nothing but religious maniacs was more than I could bear.

Of course, if it turned out that the Believers were right, it would mean they *weren't* maniacs.

Unfortunately, that didn't make the thought of spending the rest of my life with them any more appealing.

Don't think that just because I was consoling myself with the thought that this was only two weeks and therefore I could live through it that I went "gentle into that good night," to use a line my English teacher kept throwing at us last year.

I went kicking and screaming all the way. Well, kicking and screaming part of the way. I also tried whining, acting sullen, calling Child Protective Services, and announcing that I was sick and needed to go to the hospital.

I didn't actually expect Dad to believe that last one. But I had reached the point where I was desperate—not only to keep myself out of this but to keep him from going as well. I did manage to delay the inevitable by two whole days. But in the end, it did no good. He was determined to go, and that meant I was going, too. Not because I couldn't have survived on my own; I wouldn't have been the only sixteen-year-old living on the streets, not by a long shot. No, I went because I wasn't sure Dad could live without me. That was partly Alice's fault. Her words *You'll have to go with him* kept coming back to me.

Of course, Alice hadn't seen the new Dad. He might

not have been able to leap tall buildings with a single bound, but he no longer wandered around like a lost soul, either. The end of the world seemed to have made a new man of him, and he went about making our preparations to leave with energy and enthusiasm.

While Dad was busy buying a tent and getting our sleeping bags, lanterns, and other equipment ready to go, I took care of some practical matters, too—such as going to the post office and asking them to hold our mail. I also got Mrs. McGillicuddy from next door to come in and water the plants.

Dad didn't bother with things like that, of course. Why should he? He truly believed that we were never coming back.

Any question I had had about *that* ended the Sunday morning we left the house to head for the mountaintop.

"Aren't you going to lock the door?" I asked.

Dad looked at me as if I was crazy. "What's the point?" he asked. Then he took his house key off his key ring and threw it into the bushes. "We won't be needing *that* anymore," he said with satisfaction.

I checked my pocket to make sure I still had my own key. Then I climbed into the car, and we headed for Mount Weeupcut to wait for the end of the world.

Welcome to Mount Weeupcut
"CUT HOUSE"

Mount Weeupcut—pronounced by the locals as "Whee-a-cut"—was named by the Indians who long ago went by in their hunting parties. Supposedly the name means "Beautiful Mountain Blessed by the Great Spirit" though modern Native American scholars say this is nothing more than a pretty legend. But we of the Mount Weeupcut Historical Society like to think that there is a "great spirit" here on the mountaintop.

That "great spirit" led Jacob McDevitt, who owned Mount Weeupcut, to build a log cabin as a gift for his neighbors in 1897. Using timber found on the mountain, McDevitt's men put up "Cut House" in a single day: from sunrise to sunset, as the story goes. He then deeded "Cut House" to the county, to be used "in worshipful ways."

McDevitt's daughter Sarah was married at "Cut House" the following year, in the "Great Hall" in front of the stone fireplace. A picture of her in her wedding gown hangs above the hearth. Twenty-five years later her daughter was wed in the same room, though by then it had been greatly expanded to the vaulted two-story room you see now. Her photograph may be found between the two main windows on the west wall.

There are four other rooms off the "Great Hall": three were used as sleeping rooms and one as a kitchen. Today, though the kitchen is still usable—a generator provides electricity and the stove is run by wood—it has not been modernized. There is an artesian well that supplies the kitchen and two outside taps and hoses for use by visitors. Two of the sleeping rooms are used for storage. The third is the camp office.

"Cut House" and the camping facilities may be rented by the day or by the week. To make reservations, write to Mrs. Claire Webb, Post Office Box 367, Greenspar, Massachusetts 01033.

Do not dig in the area.
There is a chemical toilet in "Cut House" for
    emergencies. There are three Porta Potties in
    the woods.
All garbage must be packed out.
Dogs must be leashed at all times.
There is no telephone.
Enjoy your stay.

7

Marina

I have to say this about Mount Weeupcut—it is pretty. Pretty steep, pretty wild, pretty cold. It is not a place you want to go camping. Not even in the summer.

Of course, we weren't actually camping. Reverend Beelson was very clear on that point.

"We are waiting for World's End," he said. "We are not here for a good time."

He wasn't kidding.

The very top of Mount Weeupcut—the real top—is up above the timberline and exposed to every sort of weather. Even for Armageddon, Reverend Beelson couldn't get a camping permit for more than two weeks, and not for the upper part of the mountain at all. We had to stay somewhat lower down, which—truth to tell—was just as well.

"Till the World Ends," Reverend Beelson explained from the pulpit, "we go by Man's rules. After that, we play only by God's."

So we set up Armageddon City about a quarter mile below the top, in the firs, where there is a large, elegant log cabin called Cut House.

Reverend Beelson renamed it the Temple.

In rings around the Temple, depending how soon you arrived, were the Tents of the Believers.

Everyone spoke of things that way, as if they were in capital letters. The Temple. The Tents. The Place of Greeting. The Place of Eating. Grahame called the Porta Potties the Place of Pooping, but not when Reverend Beelson could hear.

We were all renamed, too. No longer moms and dads, cousins and friends. We were the Brethren. And the Sistern. We were the Family. I bet Ms. Leatherby would have had a fit with all those capital letters. But dear Emily Dickinson would have felt right at home.

Because we arrived in the very first wave of Believers, our tents were near the Temple. "The First among the first," Reverend Beelson explained when we were shown to our places. And we each were given a silver pin in the shape of a candle to wear over our hearts.

"Did you know," Grahame whispered to me, "that tallow candles are called dips."

"You're the dip!" I shot back.

Mom gave Grahame and me the Look, which shut us both up, then she smiled at Reverend Beelson. It was her most transcendent smile, all teeth and a dimple. It was not a smile she was offering up to anyone else.

Mom and I were to share one tent, a green army thing with a door flap made of mosquito netting—not that there were any mosquitoes that high up the mountain. It was Dad's old turkey-hunting tent, and it was pretty musty till Mount Weeupcut's constant wind blew the smell away.

The boys shared an even bigger yellow-and-blue tent, with a banner that said NORTHERN EXPOSURE on the side.

"It's on the south side, actually," said Grahame, which earned him another Look from Mom.

"When the World Ends, so will that sassy tongue of yours, Grahame Marlow." Mom's voice was soft, but underneath there was a hardness to it that I had never heard before, except when she was arguing with Dad. It felt as if she were beginning to build some strange wall between her and us. A wall that we would have to climb over to prove ourselves worthy of her love, because she was never going to tear it down on her own.

Grahame walked away, muttering something about manatees and smooth brains, but he was back once it started getting dark. He was the first to fall asleep, too. I recognized his snore.

Leo shared the boys' tent only until the middle of that first night, when some owl, with a voice like the Wicked Witch in the *Wizard of Oz* movie, scared him so much he climbed in with Mom and me. Mom was deep into the sleep of the just and never heard him crawl in, snuffling a little in his fear. But I did.

"Come snuggle with me," I said. I didn't mind. He doesn't snore, like Grahame. And since he's a regular little furnace, it made things warmer inside.

At first it was work, work, work in Armageddon City, so who had time for disbelief? I doubted even God had worked this hard setting up the universe. Only, the minute I had that thought, I sent up a quick prayer. *Didn't mean it that way, God!*

As First Comers—that was in capitals, too—we had the worst of the hard labor.

"So you can have the best of it Beyond," Reverend Beelson said at First Temple. He didn't mean in Heaven. He meant beyond the Big Collapse. He didn't say "Big Collapse," of course. Grahame did.

"It's the opposite of the Big Bang," Grahame explained brightly at breakfast.

"I'll bang you a big one if you aren't quiet," Mom said, which was totally unlike her. For a moment I almost wondered who was using her mouth to speak, till I remembered that wall.

God, I prayed silently, *save my mother. Not this walled-in stranger on the mountain.* But if He heard me, He took a long time answering.

We had to help dig privies—outdoor bathrooms—which were really just long trenches. Except for the three Porta Potties out in the woods, and one chemical toilet in Cut House, there weren't any of what Mom called "facilities" on the mountain. We were expecting 144 people, after all, which—as Grahame remarked—made 36 people for each toilet. Even at home, where we had two bathrooms for the eight of us, there was often a major traffic jam. I hated to think what would happen if a bunch of people got sick at the same time.

Of course, no one but me seemed to wonder about that. Or about where these 144 people were going to come from. Our congregation only had about 50 people altogether, and that was counting the children. And not all of them had come to the mountain. "Backsliders," was what

39

Reverend Beelson called them. "People with greasy souls." And he added that at Armageddon they would be the last to die. "So they will know to the end what they have missed," he said. "But their souls, being greasy, will crackle when they burn."

That led to some major crying in the congregation for husbands or wives or children left behind. But all I could think of was that it meant there was still lots of room for Dad, should he change his mind. And for my grandparents, too.

Lead them here, God, I prayed, remembering how often the Bible spoke of God as a shepherd. Which made the Reverend Beelson some kind of sheepdog, I guess.

The trench digging was unbelievably hard to do. My back ached, my hands had blisters, and as a consequence, my tongue began to turn rough and nasty.

"Did you know," Grahame informed me as we were standing knee deep in a hole, "that Mount Weeupcut is part of the Appalachian mountain range and is hundreds of thousands of years old?"

"And did you know," I retorted, "that in two weeks God's going to blow out the candles on Mount Weeupcut's birthday cake?"

"Yours, too," he reminded me.

"Well, at least I'll *get* a birthday. Unlike the folks below."

Which shut him up good.

I instantly wondered if it was the work or the weather or the world ending that was making me so mean. I wondered, too, how that matched up with our being the good guys, the ones God was trying to save. I promised myself I would watch my mouth carefully. And my thoughts. They were not the mouth and the thoughts of an angel.

Help me, God, I prayed again. *Help me remain kind.*

"The Sistern digging," someone said, the half sentence bringing me back to the trench with a jolt. "A cistern," she added. It was a girl named Jillian, who was digging across from me in another trench. She'd been trying for about an hour to make conversation, only she wasn't very good at it and I certainly hadn't helped her any, either. She'd say these bizarre little half sentences in a tiny voice and then look up at me, waiting for my reaction.

Her thick glasses seemed to weigh down an almost invisible nose, and she carried a romance novel in her back pocket, which was not exactly what Reverend Beelson had in mind for reading material.

I knew her from church, of course. She'd been the only other girl in the Bible study sessions, and she always asked the oddest questions. Not odd like Grahame's, which were always about wanting more information. But odd in that Jillian always seemed to be asking about herself. How *she* could relate to the parables, how *she* was to understand the Sermon on the Mount, how *she* would have divided up the loaves and fishes.

I thought about explaining to her just what a cistern really is, something we had learned in sixth grade doing Foxfire projects. The way I was thinking about telling her had nothing to do with a generous spirit. I remembered my hasty prayer from moments before and tried to think how to say what I wanted while still being kind. But before I could get anything out, Jillian went off somewhere else, on a special assignment for Reverend Beelson.

Truthfully, I was just as glad. Sharing the last days of

the world with someone like Jillian was more of a burden than I was ready for—which was, in itself, a very *un*-Christian thing for me to feel.

God, please, please help me watch my tongue, I prayed.

Does guilt strengthen our faith?

Or make it less?

First Temple was the following morning before breakfast, with the Ten Families, as we were later known—though there were some unmarried people among the First Comers as well. We met in the Great Hall of Cut House, sitting on Taylor Rental folding chairs, and Reverend Beelson gave one of his fiery sermons. The place literally rocked with *amens*.

I watched Mom as Reverend Beelson spoke. Her eyes were wide open, but she wasn't seeing anyone or anything but him. She was even trembling with the passion of his words. Thinking that there were no walls around her, I put my hand out and touched her arm. She didn't seem to feel a thing.

So I looked away, gazing out of the window at where some big bird was soaring past on wide, set wings. *An eagle?* I wondered. *A hawk?* Dad would have known which, and for a moment I missed him with a longing that was as sharp and single-minded as a knife.

But then the bird circled back again, so close this time I could see that it had a white head. An eagle, I was sure of it.

Maybe it was that eagle, powerful and free. Or maybe it was that Mount Weeupcut really is beautiful first thing in the morning. Or maybe it was the feeling of brotherhood or sisterhood or peoplehood, of all of us being together for a purpose. Whatever the reason, I looked away from the window and up at Reverend Beelson and suddenly, without thinking about it, smiled at him. My mother's smile.

He stared down at me and gave a quick, almost shy little nod, before he started in once again on the horrors that my birthday was going to bring.

I sang out my *amens* as loud as the rest.

And only a little bit of my mind—the "hind brain," Ms. Leatherby used to call it when we tried to write poetry—remembered Dad as I had last seen him, standing close to the chesty redheaded woman, coffee cup in hand, his face a contradiction of farewell smile and, I thought, some sort of relief.

8

Jed

Camp Wicky-Wacky-Lastchance (my name for it, not theirs) was pretty big, and pretty wild. Not wild and crazy. That came later. Wild in the sense of lots of trees and bunnies, but not lots of normal things, like indoor plumbing.

Dad and I reached the place by following a two-lane blacktop road that slowly dwindled to a one-lane blacktop that somehow became just a dirt road. As we drove up (and up, and up) the land got rockier and the trees got scragglier. I could feel civilization fading away behind me.

I wanted to try the cell-phone on my laptop, to see if it would work this far up, only Dad had told me to leave the computer at home. "That kind of technology has led to the pollution of the spirit," he explained patiently. "It will be forbidden on the mountain."

I would have argued, but it was simpler to just pretend to agree, and then bring the laptop along anyway. But under the circumstances I could hardly use it in front of him.

"So, are these guys really waiting for the end of the world, or did Reverend Beetlebutt just figure if we went high enough we could get straight to Heaven without bothering with the dying part?" I asked at one point on the drive.

"Reverend *Beelson*," said my father. "And I would appreciate it if you would try not to be so flip about this, Jed. These are serious matters."

I went back to staring out the window. Staring *sullenly* out the window, according to my father, though since I wasn't saying anything I don't think he had a right to claim he knew how I was feeling.

Believe me, *sullen* didn't begin to describe it.

The thing is, under other circumstances I might have thought this was all wonderful. I like the outdoors, and going on a camping trip with my Dad could have been great, if not for the fact that he had gone bonkers.

Besides, staring out the window wasn't all that bad. The road wove in and out of deep forest, and when it ran along the edge of the mountain the view was pretty spectacular.

I was watching a hawk and wondering if Muriel Ferguson would be interested in going to the movies with me once the end of the world was over, when Dad stopped the car.

"Uh-oh," I said when I saw the reason why.

We had come to a wooden gate. The gate was open, but two burly guys with their arms crossed over their chests were standing between the posts, making it impossible for us to go any farther.

Mentally I took back my "Uh-oh." Maybe we were about to be sent home and this would be the end of the trip.

45

Dad didn't seem worried, though. He just rolled down his window and said, "Greetings, Believers."

One of the guys moved in close to the car. His face was lean and weathered, as if he had worked outside all his life. "What does it take to live?" he asked.

"To Believe is to be Saved," replied my father.

"Where does Death wait?"

"Death waits below. It has no dominion over the Believers on the mountain."

The man smiled and waved us on.

"What was that all about?" I asked, once they were behind us.

Dad shrugged. "As soon as people realize that the End is coming and this mountaintop is the only safe place to be, they're going to be scrambling to get up here. But the prophecy calls for only a hundred and forty-four souls to be saved, so we'll need to protect ourselves from outsiders."

I suppose that made sense, if you bought into the Believers' whole cuckoo way of thinking. Though how anyone was going to realize that Mount Weeupcut was the only safe place without one of the Believers telling them was beyond me.

Anyway, at the moment it wasn't outsiders who were scaring me. It was the guys guarding the gate that I found kind of spooky.

Them, and my dad.

We pulled in a little before noon on Sunday. (I know because I had already started my own personal countdown.) We had to park a fair distance from the main camp, in a little parking lot around the other side of a big log cabin—a huge log cabin, actually—that I later learned was called Cut House. Well, it used to be called Cut House. According to the Believers, it was now "The Temple."

When Dad and I went to pick out our campsite, we were told by a big woman that we had to pitch our tent in the Third Ring. That was because we were part of the Third Wave. (These Guys Used Capital Letters for Everything.)

Despite the way it sounds, the Third Wave wasn't a huge flood. It was just how the Believers referred to those of us who got there on the Third Day—er, third day. *Third Ripple* might have been more appropriate, since there were only about twelve of us.

You wouldn't think having a two-day lead would be that big a deal. But it was enough to give the people in the First Wave—the Ten Families, they called themselves—a major case of Attitude. (That last capital letter is all mine.)

"Do you see what your nonsense and your delaying cost us?" asked Dad bitterly.

I didn't answer, mostly because I wasn't speaking to him.

Those of us in the Third Wave did get to look down on the people who came the next day, but by that time the major ego points had already been distributed. Besides, it was hardly worth the bother, since only eight people showed up on Day Four.

Those eight meant there were 121 of us in all. I know because the Believers had put up a big signboard where they kept track of how many people were on the mountain. I wasn't quite clear, yet, on whether they were worried about actually being able to get the full 144, or nervous about exceeding the limit.

I also wondered what it would do to their math if I told them I didn't really believe. Would I only count as a fraction? Or even a minus number?

Dad and I picked out a site in the Third Ring, a process that consisted of him eagerly pointing out different possibilities and me shaking my head or rolling my eyes. When he finally found one that was acceptable enough for me to merely shrug, he claimed it.

To add to my joy, a light rain began to fall as we headed back to the car to get our gear.

We were still unloading our stuff when a little blue Honda pulled into the spot next to us. It belonged to a young couple—David and Melinda, according to the way Dad greeted them—who had a baby with them. They were both nice looking (actually, Melinda was a semi-babe), very sincere, and from my point of view, even nuttier than my father.

"What a blessing it is to be here!" exclaimed Melinda, ignoring the fact that she was standing in the rain on a chilly mountaintop with a tiny baby. "But then, you understand what it is to want to protect your child, Richard," she added, speaking directly to my father.

She snuggled the baby, who was adorable, closer to her chest. "I just couldn't wait to get little Agnes up here, where she will be safe." Lowering her voice, she added, "I was afraid we might have a problem with my mother. She wanted to keep Agnes with her. Down where the fires will come! Can you imagine?"

David put his arm around her and kissed her cheek. She relaxed a little. Even so, she had a haunted look in her eyes. I noticed, too, that they had dark circles under them, as if she hadn't been sleeping much lately.

It took three trips to carry our stuff to the spot we had picked out. On our third trip back to the car a medium-sized rental truck drove past, pulling up to the back of the large log cabin.

"Supplies," said my father, answering the question I would have asked if I was speaking to him. "We're going to need a lot of food to get through the months between the End of the World and the time when we can harvest our first new crops."

I grunted, which was my current way of saying, *Now, that's the kind of stuff that really scares me, since it means you maniacs are actually serious about this end-of-the-world crap.*

We started back on our final trip to the tent site. I noticed a group of people digging off to our right.

"Wonder what they're working on," said Dad.

"Probably a grave," I muttered, accidentally speaking out loud.

"Death has no dominion," he murmured in reply.

We started setting up our tent, a process complicated somewhat by my silence. We hadn't been at it for more than two or three minutes when this grubby little kid came wandering over to watch. He had huge, soulful eyes that might have made him look angelic, if not for the fact that he also had a bad case of snot droop. He said his name was Leo. That was about all he said, since he spent the rest of the time with two fingers in his mouth, just staring at us.

About the time we finished—it would have gone

faster, but things like this take longer when you're not talking to the person you're working with——a bell began to ring.

"What's that for?" I asked.

"Church," said Leo, finally taking his fingers out of his mouth again. "Everybody gots to pray and sing before we can eat."

My cup was running over.

9

Marina

By Third Day, at Sunday-morning Praise Service, there were so many new faces I couldn't keep them all straight, though there were still very few kids my age there. The new people were all from Reverend Beelson's other congregation, someone said, a larger one over near Boston. They'd arrived in vans and cars, and seven people came in a VW bus that had Bible sayings painted on the panels and "Sin no more, lest something worse befall thee—John 5:14–15" on the sliding door.

So I finally had the answer to my question about how we would reach the 144 Believers. And the odd thing was, I didn't like it.

I think I was most upset by the fact that Reverend Beelson had had another church all along and never told us. Or maybe he'd mentioned it but I hadn't understood because I needed to believe we were the only one, a family of a few very special worshipers.

But when I asked Mom, she shrugged and looked up at the sky. She had given up looking at me when we talked. "Reverend Beelson told us God would provide," she

said, as if reading that in the clouds. "And he does not lie."
It wasn't clear if she meant Reverend Beelson or God.

I wanted to tell her how bad I felt about it, but I found
that I was suddenly too tired to try. Getting ready for the
End of the World was turning out to be hard work indeed.

Instead I asked God, *Help me like the new arrivals.*

And all of a sudden, I realized that having more people
would mean there would be more men to take over the
digging of the ditches and the laying out of the electric
fence.

At Praise Service Reverend Beelson announced that
the Sistern could be let off the heavy stuff permanently.

Or permanently till the End of the World.

He said a work schedule would be posted and that God
had consecrated the mountain. "Henceforth," he said—a
word I'd only read and never heard spoken—"Henceforth
we will consider ourselves Angels."

He meant this literally. Except for the halos-and-wings
part.

Some of the women—to be called Lady Angels—were
assigned to working in the kitchen and keeping the Temple
clean. Some—named Lady Seraphim—got to run a day
care for the half dozen really young kids. And us big girls—
now known as Cherubs—were told to fetch and carry for
anyone who asked.

And *everyone* asked!

There were three of us Cherubs from the Holyoke
congregation: Jillian, a ten-year-old named Ashlee, and me.
And there were two more who'd come in from Boston.
However, we didn't meet them right away, because

Reverend Beelson told us at the end of breakfast that, this being Sunday, the First Families were to be given a Half Day of Rest starting right after the meal—though this did not excuse us from Services, of course. "The other Believers will get their rest on a different Sabbath," he said. "We do not have many days left to Be Prepared."

I'm ashamed to say that was the first time since coming up on the mountain that I really thanked God for anything, though Reverend Beelson urged us to do so with every sermon.

Not only that, but I cheered his announcement, my voice ringing out all alone. I looked around and saw that everyone was suddenly staring at me, and Mom turned to give me a double helping of the Look. My selfishness suddenly burned like a brand on my cheeks. I left as soon as we were dismissed, dumping my tray and its plastic cereal bowl and silverware in the appropriate bins and racing away to hide for a few minutes in the shelter of the fir trees.

O God, I prayed, going down on my knees on the hard ground, *don't let me have a greasy soul.*

When at last I felt my cheeks had stopped sending up red flares, I started my Half Day of Rest by washing myself thoroughly in the Cut House kitchen. Water had to be heated on the stove. There were no showers or tubs in Cut House, so all we could do was hand-wash ourselves. Mornings were set aside for the girls and women to bathe, afternoons for the men and boys.

It had been embarrassing at first. The older women, especially, chose to carry large pans of the warmed water into the Cut House bathroom and wash there. But by Third Day I didn't mind scrubbing in public. After all, I had little enough to be embarrassed about! Besides, our two bathrooms at home had no locks on the doors. Dad was always promising to fix them but somehow never did. I was so used to my brothers barging in on me all the time, handbathing in front of some old ladies was nothing to sweat.

Still, with each stroke of the washcloth, I found myself daydreaming about bubble baths in our old lion-footed tub. Or showers in Mom and Dad's bathroom. And in those daydreams I really began considering for the first time what the world after Armageddon might be like.

Would there be running water? Would there be heat? Or electricity? Was there a reason God wanted to send us back to primitive times?

That kind of question made me feel worse than before. I felt disbelief, like a rash, prickling at the back of my neck and wondered if anyone could see it.

Help me, God, I prayed again. *Help me to believe some more.*

And again, God heard. He blanked all the scary questions from my mind, reminding me that Adam and Eve in the Garden of Eden had had none of those things and they had managed very well.

Well, until the serpent, that is.

After that I went to read inside our tent, my hair still damp from its bowl-wash. I purposefully let the tent flap down so it would look as if no one was there, because I needed to be absolutely alone. In the three days we'd been on the mountain, I'd come to miss having any quiet time to myself.

While I read away half of my Half Day of Rest, the boys got to run around like wild men. Except, of course, for Leo. He stayed in day care on the Cut House back porch and the picnic grounds behind. That was where the Lady Seraphim—two very large women in flower-print dresses and heavy sweaters—kept an eye on the children: five little girls and Leo.

Mom was now a Lady Angel working in Cut House, cooking and dusting and washing the floors, all the while singing hymns. She called it Praise Work, and she seemed happier doing that than she had in months, though it didn't seem all that different to me from the housecleaning she'd done before for pay. The Praise Work kept her from the boys and me, though. And she let us go without a backward glance, allowing the greater Family of Believers to take over our care.

About an hour before noon Service there was a noise by our tent. One of the flower-print ladies, a Mrs. Parker, stood there, holding Leo by the hand.

"Anyone home?" she called in a forced bright voice. The kind of voice kindergarten teachers use a lot. "Your mother told me to bring Leo here."

I poked my head out through the tent flap.

"We can't get him to stop whining," she said, through a smile. Her second chin wobbled when she talked, and it was very distracting. "And those girls (*wobble*) are bullying him (*wobble*) something fierce. (*Wobble, wobble.*) Maybe (*wobble*) he best stay with you."

I took Leo's hand, working hard not to laugh at Mrs. Parker's wobbles, and he flung his arms around my legs and clung as if he'd been Velcroed there. I didn't mind, really. It distracted me from the Seraph's wobbles and besides, Leo's my favorite brother. Maybe because he doesn't say much.

"It's OK," I said to Mrs. Parker, who—without a word or a wobble more—headed back to Cut House.

"Do you want me to read?" I asked Leo. Taking his silent nod for agreement, I pulled him into the tent and started right in on some of Emily Dickinson's poems.

He never moved. He didn't even ask for one of his own books. Just looked up at me with those pea green eyes of his and breathed heavily through his mouth. When we finished the second poem, with Leo leaning against me, his fingers in his mouth, I decided we needed to get out and walk. Maybe what Leo needed was exercise. After a morning in the tent, I sure did.

Besides, I didn't like the way Leo was acting, so quiet and without energy. Of course, even at home he never said much. With so many kids older than he was, he couldn't have gotten a word in edgewise if he'd tried, as Dad likes to say. But he'd never been *this* quiet. Of course, he'd never been away from home overnight before, either. He'd been crying himself to sleep snugged up against me. For two mornings he'd even refused to eat the oatmeal that was all that was served up at breakfast in the Place of Eating. I had tried to coax him into it with stories about the Land of Oats and the Oat King, but they hadn't worked.

Actually, I couldn't blame him for not eating it. The oatmeal was lumpy and, by the time we got to it, stone cold. Reverend Beelson was now having us practice the first being last, because it said so in the Bible. And so the First Families had to wait while all the Newcomers got to eat on the early shift.

"Let's get up, buddy," I said to him. "Emily can wait. You and I are going for a walkabout."

I tried taking him to one of the Porta Potties first, but he refused to go. He'd become deathly afraid of going to the bathroom there because someone had seen a snake the night before and all the boys were talking about it.

"A bowel constrictor," Grahame had dubbed it when we heard, though it had only been some sort of grass snake. Once I'd carefully explained the joke to Martin and Jerold and Jordan, they fell onto the ground in gales of laughter. They kept telling one another the joke over and over, which didn't make it any funnier, except to them. They laughed themselves into a kind of exhaustion, then got up and staggered off around the side of Cut House.

Leo hadn't laughed at all. And after the first time, I hadn't laughed, either, because I could see how the idea of that snake scared him. So today, hungry and sleepy and constipated and cranky, he clung to me till noon, his hand sweaty in mine. Mom never even came by to check up on him. She was taking her Half Day of Rest in Cut House, reading the Bible and talking to God. Or Reverend Beelson. Which for her had become the same thing, I think.

I towed Leo around for hours, telling him stories and reciting poems, like "I'm Nobody, Who Are You," and trying to get him to be a frog to the admiring bog, like in the poem. Usually he liked that sort of thing, but this time I couldn't coax a smile out of him, or a word.

Then a fine rain began to fall and I took him back to the tent. The last thing I needed—I thought—was for him to get sick. Leo had a tendency to run high fevers, and I didn't know if there were any doctors up in Armageddon City. Or even Tylenol for kids.

On the way back we passed a newly arrived man and his son putting up a tent. It took them a while, longer even than it had taken us with the two tents; they didn't seem to know what they were doing at all. And they didn't speak to one another the whole time they worked, which may be why it was so hard for them.

Leo dropped my hand for the first time that afternoon and went over to watch. I didn't mind. They were Believers, after all. Angels. I think Leo was attracted by the boy's haircut. He'd never seen anything like it. I had, of course, since I'd been in real school through seventh grade. The boy's hair was short all around, except for a rat's tail in the back that ran down past his shoulders.

Leo stood with his fingers in his mouth, his nose starting to run, and just stared. It wasn't very polite. But Leo's only a little over three, after all. How was he to know it was a retro style and had been out of fashion for ... forever.

When the boy finally looked up, he had a sneer on his face that was something fierce, like he thought putting up a tent on a mountaintop was beneath him. Or like he was angry at simply being up here. Or like he was trying very hard to disguise some dark, secret hurt inside.

And that was when the bell for noon Service rang out.

Leo ran back to me and grabbed my hand. His fingers were wet with saliva now, since he'd had them in his mouth nearly the whole time he'd watched the boy at his tent. His hair was damp with the rain. His nose was disgusting with snot. But he looked up at me with big eyes and actually smiled.

"He Dead."

"Dead?" one part of me whispered aloud. "That can't be. The people off the mountain are dead. We Believers are going to live." For once I was not thinking about Dad. I was thinking about Leo.

And about the boy.

Because the other part of me was whispering, *He's cute.*

Even with the rattail.

Even with the sneer.

Even with the End of the World.

Reverend Raymond Beelson
to the Believers on Mount Weeupcut
July 16, A.D. 2000
Midday Service

And so now, my brothers and my sisters, my Family, we are gathered on this mountaintop while below us the Unbelievers laugh. They laugh at our folly, and at our faith. They laugh because we believe in shame in a shameless age, hope in a hopeless world, God in a godless time.

They laugh because they are ignorant, and do not understand the terror and the pain about to rain down upon them. They laugh because they do not realize that the final days are nigh, and death by fire stalks the earth like a wolf stalks its prey.

They call us the fools on the hill. The deluded ones. Fruitcakes. Religious nuts. Maniacs.

Oh, I know the terms. I've heard their scorn. And so have you, my beloved ones. So have you.

But when the fire strikes, the laughter will die and the lamentations begin. And it *will* be fire this time, not flood, for God has given a covenant that the world will not perish by flood, as it did in the time of Noah.

But He has given another promise, as recorded in the

Book of Revelations—a promise to send His fire to purge us of our wickedness.

Hear, my people, what the Holy Book has to say!

When He opened the sixth seal, I looked, and behold, there was a great earthquake; and the sun became black as sackcloth, the full moon became like blood, and the stars of the sky fell to the earth as the fig tree sheds its winter fruit when shaken by a gale; the sky vanished like a scroll that is rolled up, and every mountain and island was removed from its place. Then the kings of the earth and the great men and the generals and the rich and the strong and everyone, slave and free, hid in the caves and among the rocks of the mountains, calling to the mountains and rocks, "Fall on us and hide us from the face of Him who is seated on the throne, and from the wrath of the Lamb, for the great day of Their wrath has come, and who can stand before it?"

The Great Day of Their Wrath. Who, indeed, can stand before it? Not man with all his machines of war, nor his computers, nor his armies. Not man with anything he has, for this is the Wrath of the Lord that is coming.

10

Jed

I can't say church was worse than I had expected. But given my expectations, "worse" would have been hard to pull off.

Let's just say it was as bad as I had feared.

The service was held in Cut House. This was better than being outside in the rain, but just barely, since there were so many people stuffed inside.

Despite the crowd, the main room of Cut House was pretty neat. It had an enormous stone fireplace and a two-story-high ceiling. I would have liked to have seen it without all the people.

We started with a hymn, sung to the accompaniment of a little battery-powered organ. The hymn was "Come to the Church in the Wildwood"—which made me wonder if someone in this bunch actually had a sense of humor.

Then Reverend Beelson offered the longest prayer I had ever heard. It went on and on about the Wickedness of the World (you could just hear the capital letters in his voice), the New Day to Come, the Fellowship of the Believers, and how Those Who Scorned Us Now would regret it when they were Washed Away in the Tides of Fire.

He seemed to take a lot of pleasure in this idea, which didn't strike me as being entirely Christian, at least not as I had been taught to understand the word.

I was impressed by one thing. You could hear every syllable he spoke, even without a microphone. The man had an Olympic-quality set of lungs.

Unlike me, Reverend Beetlebutt seemed to consider the crowded room a good thing, and he spent a lot of prayer time thanking God for sending more Believers. "Soon we will have our hundred and forty-four, and be ready for the Final Hour!" he cried.

While Beelson was praying I snuck a look around. When I used to do that in my old church I could always find two or three other people with their eyes open. Sometimes our eyes would meet, and the other person would look surprised, or ashamed. Or even give me a smile. But here in Cut House, everyone except me had their eyes squeezed shut. I wondered if they were afraid God wouldn't listen to a prayer that came from someone whose eyes were open.

Finally the prayer ended and it was time for the second hymn. This one was kind of interesting, since they had taken an old tune and set new words to it. Two of the men passed around hymn sheets, but most of the Believers didn't need to look at them; I got the feeling that anyone who wanted to be part of this gang (I didn't) had better learn the new lyrics by heart, too.

The tune was "Rock of Ages." The first verse wasn't all that different from the version I knew. It was the second verse that swung off into the weird Armageddon stuff:

As the Heathen lands below
Fall to fire and to snow,
Let them freeze and let them burn,
For a lesson they must learn.

As a hymn, it just dripped with compassion.

While we were singing I spotted a girl who looked to be about my age, maybe just a little younger, a couple of rows ahead. She had thick, glossy chestnut hair that hung over her shoulders, and when she turned her head I could see that she was kind of nice looking. Big eyes. Upturned nose. That kind of thing. She was wearing very simple clothes, which was no surprise in a place like this. I wondered if she was actually a Believer or if, like me, she had been dragged here against her will.

I was hoping the answer would be "against her will." But from the way she was singing—really belting it out—I decided she must be a True Believer. Too bad. For just a second I had had the happy thought that I might not be alone up here.

The girl sure wasn't alone. She stood in a row with five younger boys and they all looked enough alike—in the way they were dressed, if nothing else—that I figured they were probably her brothers. The youngest one was Leo, the little finger-sucker who had watched us set up our tent.

Standing next to Leo was a stressed-out-looking woman I figured must be their mother. I couldn't blame her for looking stressed, since, as near as I could make out, she was dealing with this brood single-handedly. I was pretty sure if there was a father around I would have known, since *everyone* was supposed to be at the service.

Once Reverend Beelson launched into his sermon, things really got rolling. He got that group revved up with the promise of the Horror and the Glory to come, and pretty soon they were shouting "Hallelujah!" every chance they got.

We didn't do much shouting in the Methodist church I used to go to. When I heard that first *hallelujah* it made me think of the black church my Sunday-school group had visited once—which was sort of odd, since when I looked around, I realized that the Believers were all white.

Made me wonder if black folk were going to be allowed in the World to Come.

Then I wondered what would happen if I actually asked that question.

When the service was over I tried to catch the eye of the chestnut-haired girl, but she wasn't having any of it. She saw me—I know she did. Then she immediately looked straight ahead and walked past me as if I didn't exist.

Her mother, on the other hand, gave me a look that could have stopped a rhino in its tracks. And when she got close enough, she leaned toward me and hissed, "You stay away from my daughter!"

Now, I'd be the first to admit that not every thought I have about girls is Pure. Or even merely pure. And it's true I have not found great favor with every single mother of every girl I have ever gone out with. But this was the first time I had been treated like a worm for simply looking at someone.

It seemed to me that this woman was a lot more focused on sinning than I was. She seemed to think I was plotting all kinds of evil, when all I wanted to do at this point was say hello.

To make things worse, once the woman was out of earshot my father leaned over and hissed, "For Heaven's sake, Jed! Control yourself!"

I actually said a little prayer of my own then, my first since we had arrived:

Please, God—get me out of this nuthouse!

11

Marina

God sees you. He sees you wherever you are. Inside a church or outside. So I have never quite understood the hymn "Nearer My God to Thee." How can you get nearer to God when he is already everywhere?

Dad loves that hymn, though. Just as he loves the outdoors, which, he says, brings him nearer to any God that there is. Once when we were up at Franconia Notch for a weekend of camping, he pointed to some really big fir trees. "My cathedral," he said. Then he added, "My pulpit," showing us the stone outcrop that's called the Old Man of the Notch.

Maybe if our family had just worshiped outdoors instead of in all those churches Mom dragged us to, Dad might have come up Weeupcut with us. Then he would have been safe.

Of course, if we hadn't gone to all those churches, we wouldn't have found Reverend Beelson. And then we would have all been down below on my birthday—along with the other dead people—not up on the mountain with the Believers.

The problem with thinking about *maybe*s is that there is no end to them. Ms. Leatherby used to say that that kind of question is like the mythic snake Ouroborus, with its tail in its mouth.

Reverend Beelson called things like Ouroborus "myth-stakes," and Armageddon, he said, was the "real stakes." We were all supposed to laugh when he said that. But I thought Ouroborus was just supposed to be a metaphor. Something to help us understand the world better. Like Emily's poems. I doubt Ms. Leatherby meant any of us to believe there's really a giant snake chewing on its tail. Still, Reverend Beelson said that belief in God and Armageddon were the only realities, and prayer was our doorway into the real.

At the prayer service one of the Lady Angels played on a little organ to keep us in tune. We needed all the help we could get. Mostly we sang the old tunes, hymns we had already sung many times in every church we had attended. But then Reverend Beelson had us sing a new one. Or at least an old tune with some new words. Those words made me awfully uncomfortable.

Ms. Leatherby had always taught us to think carefully about a poem. "Words mean something. They are not just filler," she always said. She used Emily Dickinson's poems to show us how every single word counts.

So what could I think of a poet who wrote, "Let them freeze and let them burn, for a lesson they must learn."

I had a sudden vision of the kids in our neighborhood. Nice kids. Innocent kids. Kids who played with dolls and trucks and sucked their thumbs and had runny noses. Kids who sometimes skinned a knee or needed an extra hug.

68

Kids I had baby-sat before Mom got religion and gave it to the rest of us.

And then I thought about all the little kids in our state. And all the kids in the entire United States. And all the kids in the whole wide world.

Did they deserve to freeze and burn?

Did Grandy and Grandma Betty? Did Pop and May-mom?

Did Yoko or Sonia or Amity?

Did Ms. Leatherby?

Did Dad?

And why was this all happening on my birthday? Did God plan it with me in mind? Was I up on the mountain for a reason? Or was I some kind of myth-stake, too?

I began to shiver, and not just from any cold. *Maybe,* I thought, *maybe religion is about feelings and not about thinking. Maybe thinking takes you further away from God, not nearer.*

Ouroborus, I reminded myself.

So I forced myself to stop thinking. I made myself shout "Hallelujah!" louder than anyone else, and sing with more feeling. I got up out of my seat and danced, too. And pretty soon it didn't matter what Reverend Beelson was saying. Pretty soon it just felt good to give myself over to the wild spirit of things. To the music, to the movement, to the moment.

That's when I turned around and saw the boy with the rattail haircut staring at me. Staring. No boy had ever stared at me in that way.

Mom turned to see what I was looking at and saw him staring, too, and she drew in a hissing breath. Her forehead got hard lines across it, all the rapture dropping away from her face. She elbowed me sharply in the side and gave me the Look.

For the first time since we had come up the mountain, she looked angry and ugly.

And old.

All the thoughts I had had before—about faith, about God, about Dad praying in the outdoors, about the snake with its tail in its mouth—all came rushing back.

My face burned. Sweat ran in a little stream down my back, between my shoulder blades. My stomach seemed to drop down to somewhere south of my knees. And I was embarrassed, because the boy could see all that heat rising in patches on my face.

Even worse—because God can see you wherever you are—I knew God could see my embarrassment and knew its every cause.

So I turned my face away from the boy and sang with an ever-increasing fervor. And when Service was over, I walked past him as if I was invisible.

As if I hoped I was invisible.

To the boy.

I was *certainly* not invisible to God.

70

12

Jed

After the service, after the royal snubbing, we went to lunch: chicken noodle soup, straight from the can. Be still, my beating heart.

Having survived lunch, I planned to go back to our tent and finish unpacking.

God, or someone, had other plans.

"You Jed Hoskins?" asked a tall, wiry-looking man as I was leaving the dining tent.

I nodded.

"You're assigned to the perimeter crew today. You'll be working with Hank and Alex." He motioned to a couple of guys standing near the signboard where the number of Believers in camp was being tallied.

"What are you talking about?" I asked (*snarled*, according to my father when he talked to me about it later).

"Your work crew. Everyone works. You think you're different?"

Different? I could have listed a hundred ways I was different from the dorks and doofuses filling this camp. I was trying to decide where to start when Dad put his hand on my elbow and whispered, "Jed."

71

Which was enough to derail me. I decided to go along with things. Not—let me make it clear—because my father wanted me to. But the fact that he'd stopped me before my mouth launched into gear meant I'd been able to rethink the situation.

The way I figured it was like this: I was stuck here for almost two weeks, and I had to get along with these people. If I refused to work, there was probably going to be a big scene, which I hate. And I was going to look like a jerk, which I also hate. Of course, it would only be people I thought were jerks who would be thinking *I* was a jerk, so that wasn't as powerful a reason to go along as it might have been. On the other hand, I've found "When in Rome, do as the Romans do" to be a good survival rule.

So I joined the work crew.

To tell you the truth, it wasn't all bad. I liked being outdoors—liked the smell of the woods, and the view of the valley that would suddenly appear when we stepped from between the trees. In the distance I could hear noises from the camp that made it seem kind of homey. And for a pair of religious nuts, Alex and Hank weren't bad.

Alex, who said he used to be a gym teacher, carried a pair of rubber eggs in his pocket. Whenever we stopped to take a break he would practice tricks with them—like hitting himself on the head with one and then having the other one pop out of his mouth. It was kind of dumb. Actually, it was extraordinarily dumb. But it cracked me up every time he did it.

We spent the afternoon—and most of the next day, too—"marking" the perimeter of the camp. If we were wolves or something, we could have just peed on the right spots. Since we were human, I had to fetch and carry and lug and tote for Hank and Alex, who were pounding tall stakes into the ground to indicate boundaries that people should not cross. I had a suspicion our camping permit probably didn't include this kind of thing. But people who think the world is going to end in two weeks don't worry much about rules and regulations.

"Are these boundary lines for us, or for the outsiders?" I asked at one point.

"What do you mean?" asked Alex. He was the larger of the two, tall and broad shouldered. And even though he was only twenty-seven (I knew because Hank had asked him at one point) he was almost totally bald.

"Well, is this supposed to be a line *we* don't cross, or is it to warn outsiders not to come in?"

"What difference does it make?" asked Hank, mopping his head with a red bandanna. With his lined face and full head of stone gray hair, Hank looked to be about fifty. He didn't like direct questions, but from things he said while we worked I got the feeling he had been a farmer until he went bust and had to take a factory job, which he hated. Now he spit out of the side of his mouth and said, "Reverend Beelson told us to put up a fence, so we're puttin' up a fence."

"No, it's a good question," said Alex. Turning to me, he continued, "I suspect the answer is 'Both,' Jed. We don't want our people, particularly the young ones, wandering too far from camp. But there's going to be people trying to get in, too. So we need to start setting our borders."

"I thought everyone was welcome," I said, mostly to see what kind of response I would get.

73

Hank snorted. "Everyone is most certainly *not* welcome. The Lord has offered exactly one hundred and forty-four spots for salvation here, and most of those spots are already taken. Thing is, as the Day draws near, you're goin' to see a lot of Unbelievers change their minds and start headin' this way." He spit again. "Be like the people who laughed at Noah while he was buildin' the Ark suddenly wantin' to climb aboard once the water started to rise. Only, there won't be any water this time, boy. Just fire. *Lots* of fire!"

He chuckled, as if the idea amused him.

Alex tried to hide his reaction to Hank's laughter, but I could tell he was disgusted. I wanted to ask if *he* really believed all this stuff.

Only, somehow it didn't seem like the right time.

Like I said, they were nice guys.

But they still made me nervous.

If the work had been a little more demanding, it might have helped me forget about the girl I had seen at Temple, which was what I had decided to do. For one thing, she was clearly a total snob. Besides, there were plenty of girls at home I was interested in. And we weren't going to be up here that long anyway. Once the Day of Doom had come and gone and Beelson and his loonies figured out the world wasn't going to end on schedule, this nonsense would be over and we could all go back where we belonged.

But you know how it is: As soon as you decide to forget something, your brain comes to the conclusion that it's the most fascinating thing in the world.

So I spent most of the afternoon—when I wasn't actually talking to Hank or Alex—thinking about the girl.

Or, to use Believer talk, the Girl.

And her Chestnut Hair.

It didn't help that the work I was doing only took about one percent of my brain, leaving the rest free to cause trouble. Times like that, my brain can get so ornery and out of control I begin to wonder if Reverend Beelson is right and we really are naturally sinful.

Or, at least, if I am.

For example: Sometimes at night I used to imagine whatever was bad about me as a kind of shadow in my body, and try to drive it out. The weird thing was, I could never get rid of it all. I mean, I could get this image where almost my entire body was clear. But there would be this one spot, like maybe in my big toe, where the darkness still clung to me. Even though it was just something I was imagining, my brain absolutely would not do what I told it to.

It was the same thing now with the girl. The more I told myself not to think about her, the more my imagination kept flashing her picture at me, coming up with scenes where we started to talk, where she turned out to be friendly after all, where we found we had a million things in common.

The thing I want to know is, if you tell your brain not to do stuff like that and it keeps doing it anyway, does that mean your mind has a mind of its own? And if it does, then who's in charge here, anyway?

It's a wonder we're not *all* lunatics.

13

Marina

Lunch was no better than breakfast, a cold, greasy affair.

Greasy. There was that word again.

If God was helping me believe, He was sure going about it in a peculiar way.

"Camel and the needle's eye," I whispered to myself, remembering the parable, which was one of my favorites. I was looking down at what had been served. It was chicken noodle soup that had gone lukewarm, with something oily and unappealing floating about like the amoebas we had watched through the microscopes in seventh-grade biology.

"Needless?" Jillian asked. She was sitting to my right. On Leo's right. But she addressed me over his head. She was trying to make conversation, but as always she spoke in what Ms. Leatherby used to call "sentence fragglements."

Ignoring Jillian didn't seem to work, but it was the most charitable thing I could do. Shifting away from her, or getting up and walking to another table, would have been both unchristian and rude. Not to say difficult, with Leo in tow. Since Mom was working in the kitchen, I was still in charge.

Jillian was nothing if not persistent. She tried again. "Needless?"

"Needle's eye," I said. "Not 'needless.' "

"And what's?" she asked.

Suddenly I didn't have the patience to be kind. I answered her in the same fragglements. "Christ!" I said. "Rich men! Camels!" Then I got up from the table. "In your eye!" I pulled Leo, pale and unhappy, up with me, and we walked out of the tent, even forgetting to dump our trays.

I dragged Leo to Cut House and up the back steps into the kitchen.

"Mom!" I shouted in through the screen door. And when she finally came out, urged by her fellow Lady Angels, I was abrupt. And nasty. Two things I'd never been before.

God, I thought to myself, *certainly works in mysterious ways.*

"I have things to do," I said. "And Leo needs a real mom for a change."

Mom took Leo by the hand, dragging him reluctantly back to the wobbles lady, anger doing for her what transcendence had not—making her remember she had a family.

And I got to go off. Alone.

Of course, I didn't really have much to do at all, except be invisible. And I did such a good job at that, I actually got out of work for the entire rest of the afternoon. I practically skipped back to our tent. All I could think of was relief—and Emily Dickinson.

The tent was stuffy, having been cooking in the sun without any shade. I opened the flap and hoped for a breeze, then settled down to read. My fingers stuck to the pages of my book. My hair stuck to the back of my neck.

After a half hour of being invisible in a stuffy tent, I was feeling clammy and strange, like on the day before coming down with the flu. Every poem I read sounded like a scold: "Departed—to the Judgment—A Mighty Afternoon—" And "I'm banished—now—you know it—How foreign that can be—"

It took me a while to understand what was wrong. But then I finally got it.

I was cheating.

I was slipping away from the hard work of being a Believer. Of course, no one else on the mountain knew it. But God and I did. And so did Emily! So I left the tent's salvation and actually walked around camp, hoping I'd be handed a job. *Any* job.

But no one seemed to notice me. It was as if I really had become invisible.

I'd just about gotten to the point of asking someone for something to do when, without knowing exactly how it happened, I picked up three other girls, jobless Cherubs just like me.

One girl was Jillian. The other two were Newcomers from the Third Wave. All I knew about them was their names. Zondra and Tiffani—"With an *i*!" They seemed to be best friends already. Or perhaps they knew each other from the Boston congregation. Either way, they were awfully cozy together, finishing each other's sentences. That kind of thing doesn't happen just overnight.

"Better here than . . ." Zondra said.

"... Down below," Tiffani said.

"With the Unbelievers," Zondra said.

"With the Fried," said Tiffani. And then they giggled, their voices in the exact same key.

"Who'd have guessed?" Jillian tried to enter their conversation in her wispy voice. "A mountaintop? Cold? July?" It was the sort of thing an old lady might have said if she spoke in fragglements. Jillian *really* had no sense about these things.

Zondra, whose dirty-blond hair waterfalled above her head from a colorful tie, gave a snorting, horsey kind of laugh. "You think this is cold, be glad the Rev didn't choose..."

"... Mount Washington," Tiffani said.

"There's blizzards there in July," finished Zondra.

Jillian stared and mouth-breathed at them. "In? July?" They nodded.

All of a sudden, without any warning, Jillian turned toward me, her eyes so magnified behind the glasses they looked big and beautiful but, somehow, trapped. "Do you?" she asked slowly, hesitantly. "Marina? Believe?"

It was as if she had spoken God's thoughts to me aloud. In fragglements. A chasm of silence opened between us, and for a long, ugly moment, I could not answer her.

"Believe?" I repeated. And then, purposely misunderstanding her, I said, "About Mount Washington in July?" I nodded. "Been there with my dad."

"Believe?" she said again, shaking her head. "About Armageddon. About the." Her eyes blinked behind the glasses. "End of the World?" Her voice was bigger than it had any right to be. And spookier.

I wanted to shout out my belief: *Yes! Hallelujah! Amen!* I

wanted to shout out my disbelief: *No! No way! You have got to be kidding!* But neither sentiment rose to my lips, for in my heart all I heard was a wishy-washy answer in a tinny, tiny voice: *Maybe.*

And then, before I could actually answer Jillian, Zondra laughed again, which made her waterfall hair jiggle uncontrollably.

"Of course Marina believes. Why else'd she be up the Cut, peeing in a trench?"

"And parked up here Praising in the cold?" added Tiffani. Their voices were flat and rough, with that long *a.* They sounded like city girls—South Boston, I thought. Ms. Leatherby would have fixed their language soon enough.

Jillian rounded on them. "How can you *say* that?" Amazingly it was an entire sentence.

"Say what?" asked Tiffani-with-an-*i*, leaping to defend her friend. "You crazy or sommpin." *Sommpin.* That's how she pronounced it.

"Gotta be crazy for God, being up the Cut," said Zondra. She waved her hands about.

"That's us!" Tiffani added. She put her arm around Zondra's waist and they went off, laughing at some joke neither Jillian nor I understood.

Jillian took off her glasses and wiped a hand across her eyes. Without magnification, her eyes were squinty little things, barely a knuckle's width across her tiny nose. "I thought," she said, more to herself than to me. "That all of us." She paused. "Believers together. Would. Make things different."

"Things *are* different," I said.

"Not. For. Me." She turned and walked away.

I suppose I could have chased after Zondra and Tiffani, but they seemed so tight together. And I sure didn't want to spend more time with Jillian. So I went back to being invisible, which has its good points. It meant a kind of escape. From my wishy-washy heart, if nothing else. And as Emily says, "I never hear the word *escape* without a quicker blood."

God couldn't say I hadn't tried.

I wandered the camp perimeter until supper, trying to look as if I were on a Cherub's errand. I must have succeeded. No one bothered me.

And after dinner—which was hot enough, because Reverend Beelson had decided food should now be first come, first served—I started wandering again. I wandered until it was time for evening Service, as if by walking I could solve my growing ambivalence, or maybe God would give me a hint as to how to feel, or what to believe.

A signal.

A sign.

A burning bush.

Or maybe one of the grown-ups could put it to me plainly. Why *we* should be saved and not anyone else. Not my pen pal in Japan, not my grandparents, not my dad.

What made us better? What made us Angels? Was it as simple a thing as belief?

Then what would happen if I stopped believing altogether?

Sometimes I think I just plain think too much.

81

CAMP SCHEDULE

REMEMBER THAT WORK IS PRAYER MADE VISIBLE

7:30–9:00	Lady Angels (1), kitchen detail
8:00	First Service of Praise
8:30	Breakfast, three sittings
9:00–12:00	First Work Session
	Angels perimeter walk, digging detail
	Lady Angels (2), kitchen detail through lunch
	Seraphim open Littlest Angels day care
	Cherubs on call all day
12:00	Service of Thanksgiving
12:30	Lunch, three sittings
1:30	Lady Angels (3), kitchen detail through dinner
2:00–6:00	Second Work Session
	Angels perimeter walk, construction, trucks
	Lady Angels (1), kitchen detail clean-up
	Seraphim with Little Angels day care
	Cherubs on call all day
6:00	Second Service of Praise
6:30	Dinner, three sittings
7:30	Service of Recommitment
8:00	Bible Study Groups
	Men in Temple Sanctuary
	Women in Temple kitchen
	Cherubs to baby-sit when necessary
9:00	Convocation of Angels
10:00	Lights-Out

SERVE THE LORD WITH JOY

14

Jed

On Monday I helped build a shed.

I have to tell you, it felt good to swing a hammer out in the open air, to lift a wall, nail down a roof, and most especially to stand back at the end of a day and look at a shed that hadn't been there that morning and say, "I helped make that!"

Of course, I could have done with a few less cries of "Thank you, Jesus!" as we worked. But all in all it was better than diagramming sentences. And it could be truly hilarious to watch one of these guys try to figure out what to say when he whacked his thumb with his hammer.

"What's this shed for?" I asked during one of my breaks.

"Storage," said Alex. "We're going to need a lot of food to get us through the Time of Troubles."

David, the guy who had come up with the little baby, was working with us that day. "Alex is right," he said. "After all, it will be another year before we have a full growing season."

I groaned. "A year of eating canned food? You'd

think God could have timed Armageddon better than that!"

David looked shocked, but Alex had already grown used to this kind of comment from me. "You'll be glad enough of those cans when the time comes," he said, pulling one of his rubber eggs from behind my ear. "Come on, let's get back to work."

I peeled off my shirt. Even though it was cool up there, the work was enough to keep me warm. I figured if nothing else, I could come back from the End of the World with a decent tan.

Another of my jobs was to help unload the afternoon supply trucks.

"Do we really need all this stuff?" I complained once.

"Won't be much usable lumber left below after the fire," said Alex, with a shrug.

We were also bringing in seeds and gardening tools. And tanks of gasoline. "For the generators," explained Hank. "For when we turn on the fences."

I thought they might have been smarter to bring up a few tractors as well. Not that we could plant much up on the mountain. But they would be useful when we went down the mountain again, since any tractors down below would have been burned up by that time. At least, according to their theory.

When I asked about it, Alex said, "The New World will not be one of technology. We will live in greater harmony with the world, just as God planned."

"Well, what about animals?" I asked. "Shouldn't we be bringing in two of every kind, or something like that?"

That actually stumped Alex for a minute. Then he

shrugged again and said, "God knows what He's doing. I'm sure He'll take care of it."

There was one more thing we were bringing in: wire. Lots of wire.

Enough to string around the entire camp.

I knew it reached around the camp because I was part of the crew that did the work, attaching it to the fence poles I had helped Hank and Alex put up my first day there.

The fencing was heavy-duty stuff, a diamond mesh made of crisscrossing wires with some nasty barbs on them. We used heavy gloves to do the work.

Along the top of the fence, spaced out about every three feet, was a series of red plastic ovals.

"What are these for?" I had asked, the first day we were working with the stuff.

"They're warning indicators," replied Alex. He paused, then added, "For when we turn on the electricity."

All this hard work didn't bother the Believers. It was practice of a sort. The World to Come was going to be a lot of hard work.

Reverend Beelson preached about it a couple of times.

"The World we are about to enter, the World after the Fire, will be a new Eden. But it will not be a simple Eden. What was can never be again. Paradise this time around will not be an easy place to live. It will be sweet and good, but it will require the sweat of our brows and the strain of our backs to make it bloom."

My version of Paradise was considerably different. It included unlimited free access to the Internet; thick, juicy burgers on demand; and parents who stayed with their kids.

I didn't figure either of us was going to get what he wanted. But unlike me, the Reverend and his Believers were expecting their version of Heaven on Earth to come true, expecting it hard and deep.

By the end of our fourth day my arms were sore and my back was aching, so supper—chicken and biscuits—was a welcome relief. And eating outside always makes food taste better anyway.

"Churchwomen are good cooks," said Dad, appreciatively. "Especially those Lady Angels."

Mom had been a good cook, too. But I couldn't remember him ever mentioning it.

We had more church after supper, with a long sermon from Reverend Beelson. He talked about wars and earthquakes and floods as signs that the End was coming. Which made me wonder if he had somehow managed to not notice that wars, earthquakes, and floods had been going on since the beginning of history.

But I didn't say anything.

It wasn't worth the effort.

After the service Dad went to a men's meeting at Cut House to talk about strategy. It sounded like a bunch of big kids playing war games to me, but he was really excited about it. Sometimes I suspected that when he was a kid he had always been the last to get picked for a team, and that he'd never gotten over it.

Actually, I was glad he was going to the meeting, since

it created a perfect chance for me to get a little time to my-self. I waited five or ten minutes after he had left, then pulled my laptop out of its hiding place, put it in a back-pack to make it less conspicuous, and slipped out of the tent.

There was no one around. I walked away from the tent, moving quickly but not running, then left the camp and headed up the mountainside. As I got higher, the trees started to thin out. Before long I crested a small rise, then went a few yards down the other side, which put the camp out of sight behind me.

Far below, the lights of the valley twinkled invitingly. Closer, like a wall cutting me off from those lights, was the fence. I couldn't see it, but I knew it was there. After all, I had helped build it.

I found a comfortable spot under a pine tree and switched on the laptop. I planned to call my buddy Howard later with the cell-phone function; he was the only one I had told where I was going, and I wanted to give him an earful about this place. But I felt like doing a little listening first, so I set the laptop on Radio Pickup. I wished I had brought my earphones; even though I was a good distance from the camp, I didn't want to chance anyone hearing me. This was a "devil's tool," after all, and way forbidden up here. As it was, I just set the volume real low and hunched over the machine.

It was kind of weird to be sitting on top of the moun-tain, smelling the pine trees, looking out at the starriest sky I had ever seen, and then bending over my little computer to get a bit of sound from the outside world. I couldn't lis-ten too long, of course, since I didn't want to wear my bat-tery down. I had no place to recharge it up here, so I was going to have to make it last for a while. But still I was eager to get a little dose of downmountain sanity.

After a while I picked up WARM, from over in Springfield, which I used to listen to sometimes at home. Dave and Big Jim, the dueling deejays, were doing their usual thing, picking on each other while they riffed on stuff they pulled from the day's newspapers.

"Here's a good one!" cried Dave. "Seems there's a bunch of woo-woos camping out on top of Mount Weeupcut."

"Bad place to get a tan," said Jim.

"No tan, but no burn, either, according to them. Seems they're up there to wait for the end of the world. According to their fearless leader, the rest of us have less than two weeks to repent! Personally, I'm planning on waiting until the last day. My theory is, sin like crazy while you have the chance, then repent at the last minute."

"You always did want to have your cake and eat it, too," said Big Jim. "Hmmm. What do you suppose they're eating up on the mountain? Angel-food cake?"

"Wonder bread and holy water," shot back Jim.

I felt my stomach twisting. Reverend Beelson had been a local joke among the Unbelievers—which is to say among almost everyone in our area—for a while. But if we were getting into the papers, that local joke might quickly become a national laughingstock. I had a sudden vision of what the late-night shows might do with this news.

It wasn't pretty.

Dave and Big Jim rolled into a long riff about what might be on the camp menu. It was pretty funny. But even though I agreed with most of what they said, it also annoyed me a little, because I knew that some of the people they were talking about—people like Alex and Hank—were basically nice guys, even if they were religious nutcases.

About the time that I thought it couldn't get any worse, Dave and Big Jim played an interview they had taped earlier in the day with some professor from up at the university who specialized in "fringe religions."

Oh, God, I thought. *How am I ever going to live this down?* God did not choose to answer.

Dr. Arlen Saunders
From "The Dave and Big Jim Show,"
WARM Radio
July 19, 2000

DAVE: Dr. Saunders, what can you tell us about these people camping out on Mount Weeupcut? Do they know something we don't?

DR. SAUNDERS: Well, they *believe* something you don't, Dave. But you know, it's nothing new. Millennialism—

BIG JIM: Mill-and-what-ism?

DR. SAUNDERS: Millennialism. It's the belief in a period of grace and happiness that is to come sometime in the future. You hear it in the phrase "Come the millennium."

DAVE: Wait a minute, Doc. These guys are talking about the end of the world, not peace, love, and freedom.

DR. SAUNDERS: *(laughing)* Actually, they *are* talking about peace, love, and freedom—but for a very small group of people. They just have to live through the end of the world as we know it first. There's a lot of things that get jumbled together here, Dave. It's magical thinking, with magical numbers: three, seven, nine. A hundred and forty-four.

BIG JIM: A hundred and forty-four? Are you making another gross joke, Doc?

DR. SAUNDERS: *(sighs)* I may be accused of gross negligence for appearing on this show. But yes, a hundred and forty-four is indeed a gross. It also has a certain mystical resonance, being a dozen times a dozen. Three and four are both sacred numbers. Multiplied times each other they give you twelve, which is the number of the apostles, the tribes of Israel, the gates of Jerusalem, and the signs of the Zodiac. So a dozen dozen carries a certain weight for some people. But the most important number in all this mix is a thousand. Technically, a millennium is a thousand years, just the way a century is a hundred years. But the word has a couple of other meanings, too. I already mentioned one of them, a kind of golden age of happiness. There's a more specific religious version: The Millennium is a period of a thousand years during which Satan will be bound and Christ will reign on Earth.

BIG JIM: Uh-oh.

DAVE: Yep, you're in trouble, buddy.

DR. SAUNDERS: Thing is, it all mixes together in people's minds. A millennium being a thousand years, and this year being the end of the second millennium of the Christian era, some people have got it into their heads that this is the time for that more specific Millennium. Setting aside any religious issues, for a variety of reasons this belief involves both bad math and bad history. In fact, we may well have passed the real two-thousandth anniversary of the

birth of Christ three or four years ago. Still, this
year has a certain appeal—

DAVE: To who?

DR. SAUNDERS: Oh, people who feel the world is out of
control, people who think—

BIG JIM: *(honking horn)* World? Hell, this sound booth is
out of control!

DR. SAUNDERS: You know, I don't know why I ever agree
to talk with you guys.

DAVE: Because we love you!

BIG JIM: And you love us! Besides, you're our resident
wacko whacker. We need you to keep us sane.

DR. SAUNDERS: You need more than me. Anyway, as I
was saying, millennialist belief appeals to people who
feel that the world is spinning out of control. Also to
people who feel that the wicked need to be pun-
ished.

DAVE: Hey, I take that personally!

BIG JIM: Waiddaminnit! Waiddaminnit! I thought you said
the millennium was supposed to be a thousand years
of peace, love, and cherry pie.

DR. SAUNDERS: Well, it is. But you have to live through
Armageddon first.

DAVE: Armageddon tired of all this hooey.

BIG JIM: Ignore that man behind the curtain. Actually,
we don't have a curtain, but this is radio, so it
doesn't matter. So what's Armageddon, Doc?

DR. SAUNDERS: The end of the world.

DAVE: Oh, great. And I was gonna learn to dance next
month.

15

Marina

The thing about signs from God is that you can never be sure.

In the morning, going to the Porta Potti, I saw a deer. There was also a dead pigeon being a smorgas-bird for crows near the perimeter when I went with a message for an Angel. And the shed skin of some small snake that Grahame had collected.

If those were signs, what did they mean?

God loved me?

God hated me?

God didn't care?

I was so occupied with my own private theology that the day sped by unheeded. I ran Cherub errands, ate the food cold or warm without noticing, sang hymns in Cut House, held Leo's clammy hand when he refused to go again into Care.

I saw more signs than I can remember.

The moon was still shining like a pale penny at noon.

There was an eagle wheeling overhead at four.

A pair of bluejays squabbled in a fir tree when I came out of the Place of Eating after dinner.

God was saying yes?

God was saying no?

God wasn't speaking at all?

I wrestled with all these questions until well after evening Service. Leo went to sleep early, but I couldn't just stay in that tent when all around the chatter of camp was still going on and the chatter in my head was louder still.

"You baby-sit Leo and the boys tonight," I told Grahame. "For a little while. Please. I have to get some air."

Actually I needed answers more than air, but how could I tell him that?

"What'll you give me?" Grahame asked.

He knew there wasn't anything I *could* give him. We had little enough up on the mountain. Except maybe a fact about something.

Then I remembered overhearing two of the Lady Angels talking at lunchtime, complaining a bit about the Porta Potties. And one of the men had leaned over, saying, "It ain't so bad, ladies. I read in a magazine that a U.N. study showed half the people in the world don't have toilets, or even a decent latrine."

So I gave that fact to Grahame, and he was so pleased he said, "Stay out as late as you want. But what should I tell Mom you're doing if she comes back and asks?" Because Mom was up at Cut House, as usual, at a women's Bible study group.

"Tell her I'm using one of the world's few toilets!" I answered, and was rewarded with a giggle from Grahame as I left the tent.

It was about nine o'clock but still light out. Some

evenings the sky is the color of smoke; this time it was more like a smear of yellow.

I was trudging through the rings of tents, out to about the Third Ring, thinking about signs, when I saw a Third Wave woman nursing her baby in front of a small tent. She was a blond, almost pretty. She didn't look an awful lot older than me. As old as my mom had been when I was born, maybe. Shadows spilled over her shoulders like a widow's shawl.

"No room in the inn?" I said, trying to make a joke. Or trying to find out where she fit into the plan. But what I said was so lame, I realized I was starting to sound like Jillian. So I gave her a big smile to make up for it.

She stared up at me with such a look of unbelief—like I was a creature from another planet or worse—that I went on by without saying anything more, the smile still pasted across my mouth.

For the first time I understood what Jillian felt like every day. Some sort of outcast. I'd always relished being alone—not apart. But apart was what I was feeling now.

I walked past the last tents and headed up toward the treeline, where the path braceleted the mountain. I walked up and up, and at last crested a small rise. The valley spread out in the distance, far enough away so that I couldn't distinguish any particular town, just a steeple here or there sticking out above the rest of the roofs, like exclamation points in humanity's sentence. The sun was going down behind the steeples a ribbon at a time, just like in an Emily Dickinson poem.

Finding a stunted pine tree, I sat down with my back against the rough trunk and watched till the sun was entirely gone and the stars winked on one by one by one. It was the kind of miracle that I could understand, an everyday miracle, the kind Emily Dickinson had so loved.

What I suddenly realized was that it wasn't God's *signs* I couldn't read. It was God's *intentions*. I mean, why should He want to end that kind of miracle in fire? It didn't seem right. Or wise. Or fair. And surely if God was anything, He was all those things: wise and fair. And right.

I was still sitting there when the boy with the rattail came over the hill and hunkered down by another pine. He never saw me and I didn't wave, remembering Mom's Look and the heat on my cheeks when I'd walked past him at Service.

He began to set up some kind of computer on his lap, which was really odd, since computers had been outlawed upmountain.

Invisible in the tree's black shadow, I didn't need to blush.

But I did.

And since I didn't want the boy to know I was watching, I didn't warn him, even by so much as a cough, when Reverend Beelson, like God Himself wrapped in a thundercloud, came up behind him and stood on the rise.

16

Jed

Sometimes I wonder about this instinct stuff. For example, when you're startled your instinct is to jump and squawk, right? But if you think about it, that's a pretty stupid reaction. I mean, what kind of a survival tactic is it to make yourself obvious before you're sure you've even been spotted?

To put it another way: If I had used brains instead of instinct, I would have kept silent when I noticed Reverend Beelson standing on the ridge behind me. But the noise that escaped my lips was enough to attract his attention, and soon he was ambling down the slope in my direction. I killed the sound on the laptop and glanced around for someplace to hide it. No luck. I was in the open, and caught red-handed.

"Out kind of late, aren't you, young man?" asked Beelson when he was a few feet away. His voice was deep and powerful, warm as a blanket, even when he was speaking softly.

"I was restless," I said with absolute honesty. "And I decided to come out and look at the stars." That wasn't quite as honest; I had only decided to look at the stars once I got up here and realized how bright they were.

Reverend Beelson nodded. "It surely is a beautiful night. Mind if I sit down for a bit? You're Richard Hoskins's boy, aren't you? Jed, I think it is."

I nodded. Then, wondering if he would notice the gesture in the darkness, I said, "That's right."

Reverend Beelson lowered himself to the ground— carefully, but with more grace than I would have expected. He was quite a bit older than my father—but not grandfather-old, if you know what I mean. He was a big guy, over six feet, with a full head of iron gray hair, cut very short. And he smelled clean. I remember that specifically, because I also remember wondering how he did it, since the washing facilities up here weren't anything to speak of.

He looked out at the land ahead of us, the stars above, the earth below, and said, "It's a beautiful old world, isn't it?"

His voice was soft, and utterly sincere. It was a good thing I wasn't sitting on the edge of a cliff, because I probably would have fallen right off. As it was I said, "Then why do you want to destroy it?"

You can probably see why I got in trouble at school so often. My tongue has a mind of its own, and it often speaks without consulting me first. OK, OK, they were *my* words, not my tongue's. But if I had thought for even a millisecond, I wouldn't have said them.

Reverend Beelson turned to me, looking as surprised as I had felt just a moment before. His brow furrowed and he asked in a soft voice, "Is that really what you think?"

I started to answer, then caught myself. What *did* I think? Sliding my laptop under my knees——I was sure he had seen it, but I figured there was no point leaving it in the open——I stared out at the stars for a while. Finally I said, "Well, I know you're not going to destroy the world yourself. But you seem awful pleased at the idea that God's going to."

Resting one hand gently on my shoulder, Reverend Beelson said, "Jed, if my son had a cancer in his leg that was going to kill him, and the doctor had to cut the leg off, I would mourn the leg, but rejoice in the operation that let my son live. That's the way it is with God and Armageddon. The Lord has seen the evil choking the Earth and knows that it is destroying the souls of His children." He paused for a moment and looked up. When he spoke again his voice was deeper and filled with joy. "But it's more than that, Jed. This is the time of the prophecies, the dawn of a New World, the beginning of something greater, sweeter, more beautiful than we have ever known. We come here in fear and in awe. We will depart in sorrow for all those who have been lost below. But beyond the day of terror waits an eternity of joy."

Listening to him talk, his voice soft and sure in the mountain darkness, it was possible for even someone like me to get caught up in his ideas. I knew how bad things had gotten. I'd seen it on TV: the stinking air, the starving people, the criminals who seemed to get bolder and more powerful by the day. I still remembered the way my mother wept when Governor Ramsey stationed armed guards in every school in the state——and how she wept again when he extended the rule that kids had to be frisked for weapons before they could enter a school all the way down to kindergartners.

I wondered where Mom was now. On some mountaintop in Colorado with her photographer, looking at the stars? —Were the stars even out yet in Colorado? It was a long way away.

For a while Reverend Beelson and I sat without speaking. Finally he said, "I noticed you have a laptop with you, Jed. You know, I'd rather you didn't have things like that up here."

"How come?" I asked, trying to sound innocent.

He sighed. "They're part of the Old World, part of what led to all the trouble, and the need for Cleansing; agents of corruption that give easy access to all sorts of wickedness."

Ah, it was the old "dirty pictures on the Internet" argument. I'd already fought that one through with my mother the month before she left with Mr. Telephoto Lens.

"Books can carry all kinds of bad stuff, too," I said. "That doesn't mean you'd want to ban the Bible, does it?"

Reverend Beelson chuckled, a surprisingly pleasant sound. "You have a future in politics, boy. Or would have, if there were going to be politicians in the future." He chuckled again and said, "And right there you can see one good thing that will come of all the pain about to be visited on the world below. No more politicians! No, nor lawyers, either."

I almost said, *Cool. Now if we can just get rid of all the ministers at the same time, it will be a clean sweep.* But for once my brain was ahead of my tongue, and I managed to hold my words in.

The thing was, Reverend Beelson didn't say anything, either. We sat in silence for a long time. When I finally couldn't stand it any longer, I said, "Are you going to take the laptop away from me?"

"Would you let me?" Before I could answer, he said, "Of course, I could probably wrestle it away from you, if I really wanted to. I'm quite a bit bigger than you are, even if my joints are kind of old and creaky. But you might choose to run rather than fight, and odds are very good that you can run faster than I can. Only where would you run to? Back to the world below? Is that computer really worth dying for, Jed?"

Like I really thought I was going to die if I wasn't on this mountaintop on July 27! But the casual way he said it made me wonder if he really *did* believe it himself.

Putting his hand on my shoulder again, he gripped it more tightly and said, "I'll make a bargain with you, Jed. You promise me not to use that machine for the next week and a half, and I won't say anything more about it. If I'm right, after July twenty-seventh you won't want to use it anyway. If I'm wrong—well, it won't make any difference, and you can do as you wish with it. What do you say, Jed? Can we make this a matter of trust between us? Will you give me your promise?"

17

Marina

When the boy turned and saw Reverend Beelson and squawked in surprise, I figured it was all over. He was going to get reamed out. At the very least he was going to lose his computer. Which, I suppose, could have been some kind of sign.

Computers—so Reverend Beelson had said in one of his sermons—were a Tool of the Old World and not to be carried into the New. Along with radios, car phones, televisions, and cameras. Which makes sense, of course. How *could* they be carried with us? There'd be no one to run the radio stations or make TV movies or fix cars after Armageddon.

And, I suppose, we were going to be too busy growing food to really care.

Actually, "replenishing the Garden" was what Reverend Beelson said. He meant the Garden of Eden, not anyone's flower garden. He's good at his metaphors. Ms. Leatherby would have been pleased.

I should have made myself known to them then. I should have stood right up and called out, *Here I am, and I am* not *eavesdropping.*

Only I was.

I didn't know which was the worse sin: listening in or not revealing myself. So in the end I committed them both. Another kind of blasphemy, but one I figured God could forgive.

Reverend Beelson spoke in his deep, moving cello of a voice, but I couldn't actually make out all the words. It was like hearing a tune on the radio but not getting the lyrics quite right. A metaphor the generation after Armageddon would never understand.

I heard, "... late ... young man."

I heard, "... beautiful night."

And then I couldn't hear anything more because Reverend Beelson sat down next to the boy and his head was turned away from me. But they seemed to sit for an awful long time not talking, just looking out at the stars.

Then they spoke some more and shook hands and Reverend Beelson stood. He seemed so big, he blotted out much of the sky before he turned and walked down the hill, right past the tree where I was trying to be part of the shadow. It must have worked. He never saw me as he went by.

Even after Reverend Beelson was gone, the boy remained sitting, motionless, his computer shut and under his knees.

And I hadn't a clue.

Well, actually I had several, but they didn't seem to add up to anything. So I did exactly what I shouldn't have done. I left the safety of my own tree, and half sliding on the loose scree, half walking, I went over to the boy.

I wasn't particularly quiet, and he heard me coming. He turned, but unlike Reverend Beelson, I didn't rate even the tiniest squawk. He just moved the computer to one side, and I sat down near him.

But not too near.

Against the starry sky he had a great-looking profile, and my cheeks went hot again, and I was thankful for the dark. I seemed to be having trouble breathing, too, which was really strange, and I didn't want him to hear that. So I kept holding my breath, on and off, which made little popping sounds. I had to give it up or sound like I had the hiccups.

"So," he said after a while. Like it was an effort.

"So," I finally answered. And it *was* an effort.

That seemed to exhaust our conversation. But the stars were a show on their own, suddenly even brighter and more sparkly than before. I stared at them and hoped for a real sentence to find its way into my dry mouth.

Nothing came. Not even a line of Emily's.

Still, the silence between us began to seem almost friendly, not tense at all. And just when I'd come to that conclusion, the boy spoke.

"Your mom doesn't like me."

"You haven't even talked to her. How do you know if she likes you or doesn't?"

"She gave me this funny look. In church. I mean—at the Service."

"She gives everybody the Look. You should see what she does to my dad."

"And then she told me to stay away from you."

"Well," I said, indicating the space between us, "we aren't *that* close."

He made a funny huffing sound, like a laugh with breath instead of sound.

I didn't know if he thought I was incredibly stupid or sort of funny. I didn't know if he was bothering to think about me at all. It occurred to me that I knew as little about boys as I did about God.

Maybe less.

He was silent for another long minute, then suddenly said, "He's not so bad."

"Who?" *Duh*—I thought.

"Reverend Beelson. I mean, I expected fire and ..."

"Brimstone?"

"Exactly." He shifted his position a little, and my heart thumped.

"He's a good man," I said carefully. "And he cares about every one of us."

"Maybe," the boy said. He was silent for a moment. "Maybe not."

"He didn't take your computer," I pointed out.

He was silent again. "No, he didn't," he said at last.

"And he could have."

The boy nodded, just a slight bit, which I could barely see. The movement made my stomach go all funny. *"Whose cheek is this,"* I thought, *"What rosy face Has lost a blush today?"* Boy, does Emily know everything, even if she never had a boyfriend.

"You *do* believe he's right?" I asked. "Reverend Beelson, I mean?"

"About the world's end? Or about something else?"

"About ... everything," I said. I thought suddenly, *God, if this boy believes everything, so will I. Completely. Without reservation. Good-bye, wishy-washy heart.*

"Well ... we'll find out, won't we," the boy said in an odd, small voice, as if faith and he had only a nodding acquaintance. I remembered in a rush Zondra saying that we all had to be crazy for God, being up here with the Believers on the Cut. The boy seemed neither crazy nor for God, and yet here he was.

"And soon," he added.

I nodded, then added, softly, "Very soon." I thought with an awful sinking feeling, *I am being wishy-washy again. Which is another word for lukewarm.* It says somewhere in the Bible that being lukewarm about God is one of the worst of all sins.

I tried to say something more, some phrase that would redeem me. Some revelation that would convince the boy. But nothing came out. It was as if I had been struck dumb.

Is this, I wondered, *what backsliding is?* Was I slipping away from God on the grease from my greasy soul?

"Beelson said we'd make a bargain about the computer," the boy said suddenly, his words tumbling out like water from a tap. "If I promise not to use it for the next week and a half, he'll let me keep it. 'Cause in a week and a half..." He stopped as suddenly, the tap turned off.

"Because in a week and a half it won't matter," I said.

"If he's right," the boy added, "it won't."

"Or if he's wrong," I said, like a traitor. It was a wonder lightning didn't strike the ground between us. I waited another second, then got up, wiped my hands on my jeans, and walked back down the hill.

I still didn't know the boy's name, but I knew something more important. It was less than two weeks till the end of the world, less than two weeks till my fourteenth birthday, and I had just fallen in love for the first time in my life.

My timing sure was awful.

18

Jed

As the girl got up to go I was torn between a desire to shout after her to stay and a desperate need to be alone for a while. In the moment that I sat there, uncertain of what to do, the choice was taken away, because she was gone.

Looking out at the stars, I had to admit that I had been wrong—she wasn't a total snob. Not a snob at all, actually.

What's her name? I suddenly thought, almost in a panic. Then I told myself not to be a doofus. There were only a few girls up here on the mountain. Finding out her name would be the easy part.

No sooner had I set aside that question than others began pounding at me. They seemed to surround me, choking me, making it hard to breathe.

I started a list, hoping that would make the questions settle down a little, make my *insides* settle down a little.

Somewhat to my surprise, the first one on the list was, *What would my mother think of her?*

I thought about that for a second, and realized that

even though Mom didn't have much to do with what was going on right now, she was always there, floating somewhere in my mind. And making a list always reminded me of her.

OK, next in line: *How did I let Reverend Beelson talk me into this crazy deal about not using my laptop?* This one really bothered me, because I wanted to believe Beelson was a nut. But if he was, then how could he sit and talk in such a calm, gentle, convincing way? If I paid attention to him, found him compelling, did that mean that I was nuts, too?

Even more frightening was the thought that maybe he *wasn't* nuts. I stared down at the valley, trying to imagine it awash in fire, then pushed the idea away. It was too terrible to think about.

OK, next question: *Was I actually going to live up to my end of the bargain? And what difference did it make if I didn't, as long as Beelson didn't find out?*

"But I gave my word," I whispered into the night air.

"Yeah, but promises to a maniac don't matter," I answered.

"But my *word* does," I said stubbornly. "It matters to *me*."

Suddenly I burst out laughing. Here I was, sitting in the dark on a mountaintop, having a conversation with myself.

And I thought Beelson was nuts!

Which brought me, reluctantly, right back to the biggest of the questions: *Was Beelson nuts? Or was God—if He even existed—truly planning to pitch a Major Hissy on July 27?*

That one alone could have kept me sitting there thinking until dawn, if it wasn't for the fact that the wind got pretty cold and I began to long for the warmth of my sleeping bag.

Standing, I took a last look at the stars. They were so much brighter here, out away from the city. I found myself thinking about how they were trillions of miles away, and how their light had been traveling for years, decades, centuries to get here.

Millennia.

Which got me thinking about the universe, and the idea that it goes on forever. That's one that always fries my brains. I mean, how can it go on forever? But if the universe does stop, if there's an edge, an end—what then? Doesn't there have to be something more, something after it?

Standing on the mountainside, under that vast sweep of star-spattered Heaven, questions like that were enough to make you start wondering if there really was a God.

I heard an owl hoot in the distance. Something moved in the grass near my feet. I could feel my blood pulsing in my temples, bringing oxygen to the billions of brain cells that were listening, watching, asking these questions.

The stars seemed to grow brighter, and I felt something seize me. I was swept out of myself, and yet was somehow more myself than I had ever been. I knew, bone deep, that I was part of the wind and the night and the stars and the darkness. Part of the owl and the grass and the questions.

I started to cry.

Not from sorrow.

19

Marina

Mount Weeupcut was not a big place to spend two entire weeks. There was only one building, a parking lot, a picnic area, the three Porta Potties, and—once we moved in—a whole bunch of tents.

We were only allowed to go a little ways down the road, and the perimeters were carefully marked by stakes with red ribbons.

The Fried were allowed to come only a little ways up.

Only Reverend Beelson and his top men were allowed to speak to them. The rest of us were supposed to be Working. Making prayer visible. And also Shedding. Shedding our sins, shedding our relationships, shedding our connection to the old, weary, worn-out, eroded, evil world.

In between there was a kind of no-man's-land guarded by the Angels.

"Angels, in the early morning," Emily wrote, "May be seen the Dews among."

And in the afternoon and evening, too. At least up-mountain.

Maybe Emily didn't know everything after all. Or at least not everything about life on the Cut. These Angels were the biggest and strongest men in camp. They were there to keep out the unwanted, the unwashed, and anyone who was not one of the 144 Believers.

Reverend Beelson was quite firm on that point: One hundred and forty-four.

Not one more.

Not one less.

He spoke of it in his sermons every day. And every day we looked to see if the number on the signboard had risen. The first three Waves had brought in only 121 Believers. But after that, each following day, the numbers told us that by ones and by twos we were getting closer to our goal.

"Do you think we're going to make it in time?" I asked Grahame when we were back at the tents.

"Numbers never lie," he said.

"Do you think we're going to get enough Believers?" I asked each of my brothers in turn.

Martin nodded. "Dad will come for sure," he said. "And Grandy. And Pop."

The twins just shrugged without answering.

Leo didn't know what I was talking about, of course. He could only count to twenty, after all. The numbers above that were as deep a mystery to him as God's intentions were to me.

I didn't even bother asking Mom.

Instead I watched the numbers rise at each new Service. Hoping and not hoping. Afraid and not afraid. Till the signboard hovered at 143.

"One hundred and forty-three," Reverend Beelson thundered in Thursday's evening Service, the end of our first week. He leaned way over the podium and waved his right arm about, his point finger waggling as if scolding us all. "And God would not save Sodom in the days of Lot for less than ten good men. See how our price has risen, O my children. We have one hundred and forty-three gathered here in the Temple. But it is still not enough. One more. Lord, we have need for one more good man."

A chant began around the Temple, "One more good man! One more good man!"

Next to me Martin started bouncing up and down on his chair, lending his voice to the chant.

"ONE MORE GOOD MAN."

What about one more good woman? I thought. *Or one more good kid?*

"ONE MORE GOOD MAN."

The room rocked with the noise.

"ONE MORE GOOD MAN."

But I was silent, thinking.

If it's a man you want, I know where to find him. At 31 School Street. In Holyoke.

But I knew shouting wasn't going to bring him here. Or wishing. My only chance was prayer.

So I prayed to God and hoped He would listen despite my lukewarm heart. *Let Dad come up. Let him come up-mountain. Let him be with us for the End.*

But either God did not hear me or He did not choose to answer.

20

Jed

I tried to hold on to the feeling that swept over me that night on the mountain, but it faded away, and I couldn't get it back.

Maybe it was too big to hold on to. But that was part of why I wanted it back, because it *was* so big. I had never felt anything like it before.

The experience did leave me wondering, more than ever, how the Believers felt. If it was anything like that, I could see why they were here.

Thursday night I decided to have something resembling a conversation with my father. He seemed to be moving up in the Councils of the Weird, or at least in the approval of Reverend Beelson, and he was away from the tent until almost midnight, meeting with the other men at Cut House. When he came back I half expected him to announce he had been made an Angel, which was an amusing thought if you considered only the words, but pretty spooky when you thought about what they actually meant in this situation.

Even spookier was the fact that Dad seemed happier and more solid than he had anytime since Mom left.

That bothered me for two reasons.

First, it seemed like his mental health was based on something that couldn't possibly last past July 27.

Second, what did believing all this stuff really say about him? I mean, given how mad he was at my mother, I could see it wouldn't bother him much if he thought *she* was going to Fry in the Fires of Armageddon (not to mention her photographer boyfriend).

But my sister?

That question had begun to bother me enough that I planned to ask him about it when he came back to the tent that night.

We had a little gas lantern, and I had it set low. I was sitting on my sleeping bag, trying to read but mostly listening—first to the insects and the birds singing their night choruses, then to the men as they called their own soft *good nights* and *peace be with yous,* then to the crunch of their feet as they went to their separate tents.

In the near silence the sound of our tent flap being pulled aside made me jump.

"Still up, Jed?" asked Dad, as he stepped inside.

Duh.

I bit back my sharp response and asked instead, "How'd the meeting go?"

Dad looked surprised, and pleased, and I realized it was probably the first civil question I had asked him since we came up the mountain.

"It went fine. They're good men."

He collapsed onto his sleeping bag with a sigh and

started to pull off his boots. "Something on your mind, Jed?"

"I was thinking about Alice."

His face got hard. "Alice is dead, son. She had her chance. I begged her to come to the mountain with us. *Begged* her. But her heart was hardened against the word of the Lord, and she would not listen."

And that was all he would say on the matter.

But in the middle of the night, when he thought I was asleep, I heard him whisper into the darkness, "Oh, Alice. Alice! Oh, my sweet baby. Why wouldn't you listen?" Then he let out a racking sob, a sound that seemed to be filled with more pain than any human being should ever have to hold.

Until that moment I had managed to cling to a faint hope that Dad didn't really believe all this—that the whole trip was just a way for him to escape from the world for a while, and that in his heart of hearts he expected to be heading back down the mountain in a week or so, feeling a little silly but ready to face life again.

But I hadn't admitted that hope, not even to myself, until that sob convinced me Dad really did believe, and tore the hope away.

I wanted to cry then, too, because somehow I felt lonelier than ever.

I looked at the other Believers differently after that, trying to imagine what it was like to truly, deeply believe that this *was* the end of the world; to believe with all your heart that everyone down below—everyone you had ever loved, or dreamed of loving, or hated, or admired, or fought with—was going to die in pain and terror when God sent His Rain of Fire sweeping across the world.

I began to search their eyes for signs of fear, remorse, sorrow.

I found it in some of them. In others I saw a kind of hardness, as if they had shut their hearts against the implications of what they believed. And in some I saw a look of purest joy. That shocked me at first. But I finally figured out that it wasn't joy at the suffering to come; they had blocked that out. It was joy at their expectation that they would see God when the New World arrived.

Sometimes, late at night, I would pretend that I believed, too, just to see what it felt like. It didn't do much good. I would get a twinge of fear, wondering if it *might* be true. But I could never totally convince myself to buy into their fantasy.

Still, I wanted to believe in something.

It was hard being the only one on the mountain who didn't.

21

Marina

The very next day, Friday, before breakfast, God answered somebody's prayers.

But not mine.

A tattered man with a scraggly beard, a broken nose, dirty fingernails, and an old army knapsack came trudging up the Cut road. He looked like he belonged more in a homeless shelter than up here with us. Sure, we were none too clean after a few days with only sponge baths. But he was filthy. He looked as if he had gone a month without taking a shower of any kind. His shoes looked like they'd walked across the entire country. But he still moved with a kind of easy grace.

When he came hiking up the road, swinging his arms and smiling, the Angels stopped him.

I saw it all from the food line, where I was waiting in front of the Place of Eating.

Two of the Angels—big men in long-sleeved shirts and jeans, the silver candle pins on their collars catching the morning light—stood in the tattered man's way. He didn't try to push through them. He just bowed his head, not like he was afraid but as if he had plenty of time to wait. All the time in the world.

Just then Reverend Beelson came out of Cut House on his way to the Place of Eating and saw them. He saw them, smiled, and opened his arms wide.

"Let him come in," Reverend Beelson boomed out. "Let him come in, for his Father's door is wide open." He went down the stairs and waited while the tattered man walked the hundred feet to him.

"Charlie," Reverend Beelson said when the tattered man reached him, "Charlie, you've come back home."

"Well, I've come back to you at any rate, Papa," said the tattered man. "It's a long hike from L.A."

"Praise the Lord," Reverend Beelson said, and put his arms around the tattered man, never minding how dirty he was. And then they sank down to the ground together, weeping.

Weeping!

Like in a movie!

And in that moment, all I wondered was how far a hike it really was from L.A., and whether falling to the ground like that hurt their knees.

We all left the food line, though, and stood in a big circle around them.

Reverend Beelson mumbled something about "lost lambs" and "prodigals" and a lot about "forgiveness."

Then they stood, and Reverend Beelson, with this strange smile that looked like he was all lit up from inside, announced, "He is our awaited. Our hundred and forty-fourth. My son, my own true son, Charles, who troubled his mother and broke my heart. But see—the Lord has washed his sins away. His coming augurs great tidings. He will do wonders. Give him welcome. We are all here now. Our Heavenly Father's door is now closed. The mountain is ours for eternity. Praise be."

Zondra and Tiffani suddenly started in on "Rock of Ages" with the new verses, and everyone joined in. Jillian, looking like she'd just won the lottery, had her hands up in the air, swaying back and forth. The people next to her were clapping and crying, and one man, balding and with a gray mustache, began leaping up as if he wanted to dunk a basketball, as if he wanted to touch the sky.

Fat Mrs. Parker, the wobbles lady, began to spin around slowly like she was dancing, only there weren't any steps. She looked incredibly happy, though, turning in place all by herself.

And Mom suddenly started shouting out some strange sentences that sounded like Polish, only she doesn't speak Polish, and as she shouted she looked up at the sky, too.

It was so embarrassing. I tried to grab her shirt, but she never even noticed. Leo got scared and began to cry and call for Mom, but she was too busy Praising, so I gathered him to me. He clutched my leg and shook as if he were freezing.

I wanted to join in the celebration. Really I did. I wanted to sing the hymn with every ounce of belief in me. I wanted to take Leo's hand and get him to dance and spin around, to be part of the whole joyous scene. Only I didn't, because Leo was shivering against me and the twins were giggling and Martin was complaining about being hungry and asking when were we going to eat.

And all at once everything felt phony. Like a bad movie

on TV that you turn off because it's too silly. Reverend Beelson's real son, Charlie, washed clean of his sins but not clean anywhere else, coming at the last minute as if he had been called—by phone if not by God. People going into trances and dances and falling-on-the-ground seizures.

Worst of all, I couldn't stop thinking about what Reverend Beelson had said: *Our Heavenly Father's door is now closed.*

Because that meant my earthly father was shut out on the other side.

Shut away from me forever.

22

Jed

I missed the arrival of the big Number One Forty-four because I skipped breakfast that morning. To tell you the truth, I was planning to skip work detail as well. Not because I was feeling lazy. I just needed to get off by myself so I could think in a way I couldn't seem to manage with all the religiosity going on around me.

Sometimes I felt as if all that praying and stuff was creating, oh, a kind of radio interference—sending static into my brain. Which was something to think about in itself, since if it was true, it meant that prayer really does have some sort of power, an idea I had dropped many unanswered prayers ago.

Anyway, even though I wasn't there to witness the arrival of our final Happy Camper, I heard all the singing and the hoopla that followed. The sound made me curious enough that I edged back toward the camp to see if I could figure out what was going on.

As I stood beneath an oak tree, watching the Believers sing and shout and dance, I was torn between thinking, *What a bunch of dips!* and feeling lonely and left out.

121

Then I noticed the chestnut-haired girl standing off to the edge of things, looking as if she felt left out, too. For some weird reason, that made me feel less lonely.

Now, while I missed the Arrival, I did get a good look at the immediate result of it. I don't mean the ecstasy in the camp. I mean something that happened shortly after that: the *closing* of the camp.

I saw that because I had been planning to leave the camp altogether. Not permanently; I still didn't want to leave my father alone with these people. I just wanted to get the mental version of a breath of fresh air. So after all the hooting and hollering died down, I slipped away again.

I found a spot deep in the woods and sat there munching some of the junk food I had smuggled up with me while I waited until everyone was busy at their jobs for the day. It was kind of nice: the air all sweet and clean, a little time to myself, the noise of the camp in the background to keep me from feeling too lonely. You could hear those sounds change as people settled into the rhythm of their work.

Beneath it all I heard a kind of hum, low and steady, that I couldn't identify.

Yet.

Once people were pretty much in place, I started through the woods toward the gate. I didn't plan to go through the gate itself, since I knew it was guarded by a pair of Angels. I was mostly using it for a marker. I figured if I wasn't careful where I crossed the perimeter fence, I might end up wandering all over the mountain, which was wild enough and big enough that a guy could get lost on it for a good long time. My plan was to cross the fence about fifty feet from the gate, then walk parallel to the road for maybe a quarter of a mile. After that I could get right on the road and ramble as far down the mountain as I wanted. I knew I'd have plenty of time to duck into the underbrush if I heard a truck coming.

I was nearing the gate when I heard angry shouting. Naturally, I was interested in what it was about. (If you think that makes me sound nosy, then try to convince me that you wouldn't have been interested, too.)

I slipped through the woods, stopping when I could see not only the gate but a Toyota 4-Runner parked on the far side of it. The driver—a big, burly guy with a red face and a neck as thick as my thigh—was standing with his hand on the open door, looking major pissed.

In front of the gate, blocking his way, were two Angels. Even from behind I could tell they were the same ones who had been guarding the entrance when Dad and I drove up on Sunday.

But one thing had changed since last Sunday.

Now the Angels were holding guns.

Big ones.

I looked twice, to make sure I wasn't hallucinating, then slipped a little closer and stood behind a tree to listen.

"I'm sorry, but you can't come in," said one of the Angels. He spoke softly, very politely, but with absolute assurance.

"The hell I can't!" shouted the man. "My wife and kids are in there, and I want to see them!"

"The camp is officially closed to Outsiders," replied the other Angel. "The last Believer has arrived. The Prophecy is complete and God's charge to us has been fulfilled."

"Well it's about to get *un*fulfilled!" shouted the man. He started toward them.

The Angels raised their guns.

123

I couldn't see their faces, because I was standing behind them. But I could see the guy approaching, and from the look on *his* face, I'd guess that the Angels' expressions pretty clearly said, *We* will *use these.*

"You haven't heard the last of this," the man snarled, his face even redder than before. Then he spun away, jerked open the door of his 4-Runner, wedged himself behind the wheel, slammed the door, made a three-point turn, and drove off, tires spitting dirt as he went.

I backed into the woods, trying not to make any sound. Now I *really* wanted to get away from these wackos. Traveling parallel to the perimeter fence—the fence I myself had helped set out—I slipped through the trees until I thought I was far enough from the gate that there was no chance the guards would see me leaving. Then I cut toward the fence, figuring I would either climb over it or scoot under it.

That was when I got the second shock of the morning, so to speak.

The red warning disks were flashing.

The fence had been activated.

Suddenly I understood that low hum I had heard earlier. When the last guy arrived, they had turned on the generators.

Give Beelson the benefit of the doubt. Say that the fence really was there to keep us from being overrun by people like the red-faced man. Even so, the opposite was true as well. The Outsiders couldn't get in, but those of us on the inside couldn't get out.

I walked along the fence for maybe another hundred yards, thinking and fuming, furious at this feeling of being trapped.

Suddenly I heard something thrashing on the ground in front of me. I took a few steps forward, then stopped, trying not to puke.

A squirrel lay next to the fence. Its paws were charred, and an awful smell rose from its scorched fur.

It twitched one final time, then lay still.

I turned and ran into the woods, not caring how much noise I made.

23

Marina

Angels with guns.

It was such a strange idea, I couldn't get my mind around it.

But right after the tattered man arrived, after we sang and gave thanks for his arrival, after the generators were turned on, their low drone filling the camp, two of the Angels went into Cut House and came out with about a dozen rifles. They handed them around to the biggest men in the camp.

And I thought, *What would God say about this?*

And then I thought, *What would Mom say about it?*

And then I thought, *What would the rattailed boy say?*

I wanted to ask him—the boy, not God or Mom—but I couldn't find him anywhere. You'd think that since Mount Weeupcut was not a very big place, we would be stumbling over each other all the time.

But he wasn't anywhere.

I wondered suddenly if he had actually run off, down the mountain, afraid of the guns.

Part of me thought that if he in fact had left, we'd be

one short of our number again and there'd be room here for Dad.

Another part of me wanted the boy within a breath space of me, even if it meant my stomach got that queasy, lumpy feeling and my cheeks went hot and cold.

But why was I feeling that when I should have been contemplating the End of the World? Especially since I barely knew him, had spent maybe two hours in my entire life with him, spoken scarcely a dozen sentences to him.

I should have been caring about what God thought.

Not the boy.

But I kept on looking for him anyway, my eyes doing what my mind tried to shun. Looking—but not finding.

I didn't see him digging ditches, stringing wire, unloading trucks that day. But then I was busy with running errands and watching Leo again.

I didn't see him at meals, at least not at any of the sittings we were at. But then there were three sittings, so maybe he just ate later than we did.

I suppose I could have asked Jillian or Zondra or Tiffani if they had seen him. But I didn't want them knowing that I cared.

So all day I tried to look without being seen, to ask without being heard, to wish without actually praying.

And then I didn't even see him at evening Service, either, when Reverend Beelson told us about our white robes. And every single one of the other Believers was there.

I looked around and around the packed Temple, trying to spot the boy, till Mom smacked me on the back of the head for looking and hissed a word at me that I will *not* repeat. But what she called me caused me to wonder even more: What was happening to our family if she could even think such a thing?

It sure wasn't something Dad would have said.

And it wasn't something Mom would have said, either, downmountain.

Despite that name she called me, despite what it implied, I couldn't help looking for the rattailed boy, trying hard not to be seen looking, until it was way past time for bed. One of the Angels came up to me. "Curfew, little lady," he said, not unkindly. I nodded and went to my tent, crawled into my sleeping bag, and just lay there, thinking.

Leo lay curled beside me, his damp little face like a pale moon and his whimpering cries painful to hear.

Mom was on the other side, making the little moans that signaled she was deep into her sleep as well. She had gone to bed without ever apologizing for what she had called me.

But how could she apologize when she no longer spoke to me? Oh, she grunted *at* me. She ordered me to kneel, to pray. She said, "Turn off the flashlight, Marina." Or, "Watch Leo and the boys, Marina!" But her soft words and conversation were only for Reverend Beelson now. And God.

So I lay uncomforted in my sleeping bag, feeling the hard-packed dirt beneath me. A lone pebble felt like a boulder under my shoulder and I moved around until it was gone. I stared up at the top of the tent, a fuzzy black against a blacker sky, and gave myself over to thought.

I thought, *His eyes are deep brown and soft. His nose is strong looking, not quite a beak. He looks like a young hawk, not quite tamed.*

I thought, *He's bright and he thinks carefully about things. Cares desperately about things. Things he knows. Things he doesn't know.*

I thought, *He's not quite a Believer but he's here. And maybe that will be enough.*

I thought, *I still don't know his name and don't know who to ask.*

I thought, *It's six days till my birthday, which is the End of the World. What time do I have for love?*

24

Jed

I slipped back into the camp in time for the last sitting of lunch. I returned not because I wanted to be with the others, or even because I was hungry, but because I was hoping I might find some chance to talk with the chestnut-haired girl.

That's pretty dopey when I think about it now. For one thing, as near as I could tell she was as caught up in the wackiness as the rest of them. For another, I didn't know how to find a place and time to talk to her in private anyway. Privacy did not seem to be a concept among the Believers. Not to mention the fact that the girl's mother would have had seven kinds of kittens if she saw me anywhere near her daughter. But I wasn't thinking about all those things. I was thinking I desperately needed to talk to someone, and she seemed like the best candidate.

Which was weird in itself. We had barely spoken the night before, had scarcely looked at each other, hadn't come near to actually touching. Yet I still felt we had connected somehow.

As I was looking for her, someone's hand clamped on my shoulder, making me jump in surprise.

"Missed you on work detail this morning, Jed," said Alex, leaning close to my ear. He tightened his grip as he spoke, a little message to let me know that he was annoyed.

When I started to stammer an excuse, he loosened his grip and said, "Forget it. I will, as long as you don't do it again. Now come on. We've still got lots to do."

I should have stayed in the woods.

The afternoon was long and hot, especially since our job for the day was digging a big storage pit for a shipment of potatoes we had coming in to help us get through the first winter after Armageddon.

"Exactly when are we going to go back down below?" I asked, when I found out what the pit was for. (I used "we" in that question just because it was simpler to include myself than to say, *Exactly when are you nuts planning to go back down below?* When in Rome, etc.)

"Hard to say," replied Hank, who was working with us again.

"It really depends on what's left when God is done with them down there," added the fourth person on our crew, a paunchy, middle-aged guy named John. He mopped his brow with a big red handkerchief. "Thing is, whether we stay up here or go back down, we're going to need enough food to get through until the next growing season."

Despite his paunch, John was amazingly strong. I'm in pretty good shape, but he could dig a lot longer than I could without needing a break.

I was working up a real sweat myself. In fact we were all pretty rank before the afternoon was half over. And my arms were starting to hurt.

131

Would I rather have been at home, playing a video game?

Probably.

On the other hand, there was something satisfying about being with the men, working on something solid. And I preferred working with Alex's crew to any of the others. In addition to those goofy rubber eggs of his, he knew an astonishing number of jokes. Even though they were totally nondirty, some of them were pretty funny. (And some were pretty stupid.)

Hank turned out to be a big baseball fan, and I spent part of the afternoon swapping stats with him while we worked.

Toward the end of the day I asked him why he bothered to remember all of them, since he believed the world was going to end. He didn't even miss a beat. "So they won't be lost," he said solemnly.

Once, when we were taking a break, one of the girls came over with a pitcher of lemonade for us.

"Thanks, Tiffani," said Alex, after he had downed a glass in a single long pull. "That hits the spot."

He patted his stomach, which was lean and hard.

Tiffani giggled.

"I'm hoping she'll be my Eve," said Alex confidentially, after she was gone.

"Huh?"

"Oh, once she's a little older, of course," he said quickly. "Reverend Beelson says sixteen is the proper age." He gave me a sly look and said, "I notice you've had your eye on that little Marina Marlow."

"Who?" I asked, trying to sound innocent.

Alex snorted. "You know who I mean. From the

132

Holyoke congregation. About the same age as Tiffani. Long reddish brown hair. Big eyes. You'd better watch out, though. You're not the only one who'd like to get chosen for her."

"Her mother doesn't like me," I said, mostly to keep the conversation going while I tried to digest this new bit of weirdness.

Alex shrugged. "Mrs. Marlow doesn't like anyone. Except Reverend Beelson, I guess. Kind of a messy situation. Her husband stayed down below. He's got a girlfriend down there, from what my sister tells me. You know how women are—love to gossip. Anyway, it's just as well. That he stayed, I mean. He wouldn't have fit in up here. But don't worry about Mrs. Marlow not liking you. The Rev will be doing the choosing."

At that point Hank threw his shovel over the edge of the pit. "Hey, Romeo," he said, speaking to Alex. "Why don't you stop yakkin' and dig for a while?"

Well, I had found out the girl's name. And quite a bit more besides. More than I wanted to know, really.

What I didn't find out was what Alex, or any of the others, thought about the camp being sealed—mostly because I wasn't sure how to bring it up without going into detail about how I had spent the morning.

I wasn't sure they were the ones I wanted to talk to about it anyway.

But as evening got closer I found I couldn't stop thinking about the gun-toting Angels and the red-faced man.

And the fence.

The image of that fried squirrel wouldn't leave me. Neither would the smell.

In some of the fantasy games I have on my computer, knowing a person's name gives you the power to summon her. It didn't work that way with Marina. At least, I didn't see her at dinner that night, despite some powerful wishing. It wasn't until evening Service that I finally spotted her, standing at the front of the Temple with the rest of her family.

Since she was right at the front, I couldn't talk to her. I'm not even sure she knew I was there. Her mother, on the other hand, did manage to spot me. I think the woman has radar.

The look she gave me was not filled with what you would call Christian love.

As usual, Reverend Beelson gave a real ripsnorter of a sermon. I have to say that even when he was spouting nonsense there was something fascinating about him. His voice was rich and powerful, and the rhythm of his language rolled over you until you were caught in the surge and the pull of it, strong as a tide, carrying you out into the sea of what he believed.

In fact, he really had me—until he started talking about having us dress in white robes for the Big Day.

Yeah, right!

I had no intention of dressing up like a weenie, even for the End of the World.

But to tell you the truth (and there's not much point in writing all this down if I don't), I found it easier to hold on to my skepticism in the bright daylight. That night, with Dad off at another men's meeting at Cut House, I flopped down on top of my sleeping bag and lay there, alone in the tent, just thinking. A light breeze was whispering through the pines above me. I could hear the murmur of voices from people gathered around late-burning campfires. Baby Agnes began to squall in the tent right next to ours. I heard her father, David, begin to sing to her, a lullaby about God watching over her. After a few minutes she calmed down again.

I began to wonder if it was possible Reverend Beelson was right.

Let's be clear: Part of me firmly believed that even asking the question was screamingly stupid.

The problem was, another part of me kept coming back to it, picking at it like a scab on a wound.

I suppose I shouldn't have been surprised. Reverend Hill at the Methodist Church used to say it was hard to keep your faith when everyone around you is a disbeliever. If that's true, then it would make sense if it's equally hard to cling to your disbelief when everyone around you is just dripping with faith.

The idea that Beelson was right would have been easier to resist if the camp had been populated exclusively by wild-eyed wackos. But even though a few of them—like Marina's mother—were seriously over the edge, most of the people were pretty nice, and pretty normal. Except for the fact that they believed this one ridiculous thing.

Finally I grabbed my laptop and crawled out of the tent. Despite my pangs of guilt over breaking my promise to Beelson, I headed up the mountainside.

I needed to know what was going on in the world outside.

Or maybe just to make sure it was still there.

25

Marina

Something wakened me. It might have been Leo scrabbling about inside his sleeping bag, or Mom Praising in her sleep, or one of the Angels checking the camp, or yet another Believer struggling to find the privy trench.

Something wakened me. I thought it was my name being called.

"Marina. Marina, sit up and see," the voice said.

I sat up and was suddenly as awake as I had ever been, as if all the times before that moment of sitting up had been some kind of a dream. I could see things I had never seen before, understand things that had never been clear before. Emily Dickinson's poem that I had memorized for Ms. Leatherby's class as part of my final exam was running around in my brain: "The Fact that Earth is Heaven— Whether Heaven is Heaven or not"—

"Of course," I whispered to the sleepers in the tent.

For the first time, I understood what Mom must have felt like when she had her revelation.

I had to tell someone. But who?

Not Reverend Beelson. My revelation was not his. Or

Mom's. Or the 143 others', dreaming the End of the World around me. My revelation was about God's love, not His anger; God's peace, not His war. I saw things blooming, not dying. A light rain, not a fierce fire.

So I got up, pulled on my jeans, tucked my nightshirt in, found my socks, shoes, and jacket, and went out.

The night was cold, but somehow that no longer mattered. The sky was a map of stars, so bright they seemed to dance about, beautiful, distant, but real. I followed that star map to the hill where the rattail boy and I had met.

I felt so clear about what I saw, I expected him to be there waiting for me, staring out at the world—the old world below that Beelson said was going to end but that I knew would not. It would have been the right, magical thing to happen, to have the boy there. A storybook would have planned it that way. Or one of Emily's poems.

But the hillside was bare.

Something inside me—that clear, still, knowing center—grew cloudy again. Whatever it was I thought I knew disappeared as suddenly as it had come, and all I could see ahead was what Reverend Beelson said was coming: fear and fire, fire and fear.

My legs felt wobbly, and I had to sit or I'd fall right over. So I plopped right down on the stony ground and for a while just looked—not at the lights below, where all the unlucky Unbelievers were, not at the lights above, where God was supposed to be, but at the black, uncharted space between.

Between.

That's where we are, I thought. *The Believers.*

And I wasn't sure it was a good or comfortable place

to be. Or an easy one. None of my old schoolmates or my Japanese pen pal were here. My dad and my grandparents and Ms. Leatherby weren't here. Sonia and Amity weren't here. Only my brothers and 138 strangers, my mom one of the strangest.

I sat thinking about that until the cold impressed itself on my bottom and I began to shiver. Shivering as much with fear and anxiety as with the cold.

So I stood and started to go back to the camp; then I stopped. I didn't want to stay between anymore. Between earth and sky. Between Mom and Dad. Between family and strangers. Between belief and unbelief. I wanted to be sure of things again. As sure as I had been before we came up Mount Weeupcut.

I didn't want to go back to the camp and the claustrophobic little tent where Mom was dreaming happily about the End of the World and Leo was getting sick with nightmares.

And I couldn't go downmountain to find my dad, because the road was guarded by armed Angels.

So I did the only thing I could do.

I went up.

I went up, with my way lit only by the stars, along a rocky path that twisted like a snake's spine, higher and higher, up beyond the treeline.

I turned around once and saw the camp below, the tents in circles, dark against dark, the lights of Cut House the only real illumination. And farther down was the world that Reverend Beelson was certain was waiting to end.

God, I prayed, *give me such faith again.*

Then I turned my back on camp and Cut House and world and all and continued to climb.

It wasn't a long way, not like going up the Rockies or the Alps or even up Mount Washington, which I'd only done in a car. A couple hundred yards, maybe. Yet in the dark, at night, in the cold, with a long drop to one side, it felt like forever.

I hadn't even reached the top, wherever the top was, when I heard something. Something I didn't recognize. Something wild. Something awful. Something inhuman, coming from a black hole in the side of the mountain. Screeches, wails, a *rat-a-tat-tat*. A hint of the coming Armageddon.

And then, suddenly, I realized what it was.

Music.

Rock music.

Right! Music coming out of the side of a rock!

I suppose it was stupid, going over to investigate. Crazy, even. But at that moment, the entire world—or my part of it, anyway—seemed stupid and crazy. I scrambled up the rocky path and made my way carefully across yards and yards of loose scree that tumbled down over the edge of a black cliff. I was pulled along by that thread of sound.

And then I saw an even darker dark against the rock-face.

The opening to a cave.

I walked over and peered in. There, close to the entrance, sat the rattailed boy hunched over his computer, his face grimly lit by the flickering screen.

"You *promised*!" I cried, my voice sounding older, colder, fiercer in the echo chamber of the cave. I put all my anger and agony into that one short sentence. "You promised."

26

Jed

I nearly went out of my skin when Marina showed up at the cave. It didn't help any that the first words out of her mouth were "You promised!"—or that those words were spoken in a voice heavy with accusation.

Frankly, it was too bad she said anything at all. Standing at the mouth of the cave, with the Milky Way glowing in the black sky behind her, she had been nothing more than a shape outlined with stars. It made her look magical. Heavenly, even. Heck, I might actually have thought she was an angel—a real angel, not some bozo with a gun—if she hadn't opened her mouth.

I bet angels don't talk much.

Anyway, I would have been glad to see her—thrilled, really—if she hadn't started off sounding like she was shaking a finger at me. Not to mention that she nearly scared me to death, since I'd been totally focused on trying to get the laptop to work inside the cave.

My first thought when I'd found the cave had been that it was a place where I would be safe from interruption. But it had turned out to be lousy for the laptop's communication functions.

140

Or for keeping me safe from interruption, for that matter.

"What the hell are *you* doing here?" I snarled—which, trust me, is not the best way to greet a girl you're interested in.

Marina backed up, disappearing into the darkness.

"Wait!" I cried, setting aside the laptop. "I'm sorry. I didn't mean that. Come back."

I wanted her back because I really did want to get to know her. I also wanted to see if I could talk her out of squealing on me.

She had stopped only a few feet from the cave. "I'm sorry," she said, in a voice so soft I could scarcely hear it. "I didn't mean to frighten you."

"I wasn't frightened," I replied, which was totally untrue. "Just surprised. What are you doing up here, anyway?"

She looked away for a minute, out at the stars. "I couldn't sleep," she said at last. "So I decided to go for a walk."

Her voice was soft and husky, and I could tell that there was more to her being up here than she was saying.

"Kind of dangerous for a girl to be out alone at night," I said.

She snorted, and her voice got stronger. "I can take care of myself. Besides, there's no one but Believers on the mountain. They're not going to hurt me."

That depends on how you define hurt, I thought, recalling what Alex had told me about the new Eves. I decided this wasn't the time to bring that up. I let a moment pass. Then, trying to sound friendly, I said, "You're Marina, right?"

The stars were so bright I could see her smile. It was just as dazzling. "How did you know?"

I shrugged. "One of the guys told me." After another minute went by, I added, "I'm Jed."

"Jed," she said, as if tasting it to see if it really fit me or not. Then she laughed, a small, silvery sound that went right through me. "So that's what Leo meant."

"Leo?" I asked, feeling a ridiculous twinge of jealousy.

"My baby brother. He was watching you set up your tent the first day you got here. When he came back, he told me you were Dead. I couldn't figure out what he meant."

We were silent again, but it was a slightly more comfortable silence now. After another minute or so I said, "About the laptop——"

"I shouldn't have said anything. It's not my business."

"No, you're right——I did promise. But I was nervous."

"About what?"

It was my turn to look out at the stars, to hesitate. "I went out earlier today, heading down the mountain." I paused again, wondering how much to tell her. "I was thinking about leaving the camp. Just for a while," I added quickly, when I heard her gasp of surprise. "Just for a little break. The thing was, I couldn't get out. They've got us barricaded."

"You mean the fence?" She set her chin and looked angry. Or maybe scared. Or something in between.

I took a breath. "Yeah, the fence. The highly electrified fence. *And* the guns."

Something flickered in her eyes, but she didn't say anything.

I didn't say anything, either, even though I'd been dying to talk to her all day.

After a silence that seemed to last for years, she said, "What's all that got to do with breaking your promise to Reverend Beelson?"

It was all I needed.

"Well, while I was trying to figure out how to slip away I saw something down at the first gate." I paused, remembering the scene. "I heard kind of a fuss, so I slipped over to where I could watch. This big red-faced guy had driven up in a 4-Runner and he wanted to get into the camp. Only, the Angels wouldn't let him. Which wouldn't have been that big a deal, except that it was kind of scary that they were using guns to keep him out. Anyway, the guy said his kids were up here, and that he would be back to get them. I also got the sense he wouldn't come back alone."

I paused and looked out into the night. A shooting star fell, blazing through the sky. It reminded me of Reverend Beelson's sermon.

"I still don't understand what that has to do with your computer," said Marina, jolting me back to the present.

I shrugged. "I couldn't stop thinking about that scene. Finally I decided I ought to see if I could find out what's going on down below—find out if there really are more people planning on coming up here. It could mean big trouble."

"Why didn't you just tell Reverend Beelson about what you saw?"

"I'm sure the Angels told him about the incident at the gate," I replied, ignoring the fact that I didn't really want to tell Beelson what I'd been up to that morning. "What I'm trying to find out now is if there's any news about *others* planning to come up here."

"And what will you do if there is?"

I didn't answer, because I hadn't worked that out yet.

The silence of my non-answer hung in the air between us. Finally Marina slid to the ground. I slid down beside her, trying to decide whether I should try to hold her hand or not. That's the scariest time for me when I'm with a girl, that moment when you first reach out. I feel absolutely naked then. Terrified, to tell you the truth.

While I was dithering, Marina spoke again. Staring out at the night, her voice soft as a feather, she whispered, "What do you think, Jed? Is the world going to end next week or not?"

27

Marina

Of all the things to say to the first boy you have ever
fallen for: *Is the world going to end next week or not?*

That's hardly a romantic question.

And romantic was what that place called for.

There we were, alone on a mountaintop under a ceiling of stars. We had gone through a couple of difficult
moments of misunderstanding and had gotten past them
without seriously wounding ourselves. We had everything
but an orchestra playing love songs.

And then I put this enormous, horrible, inescapable
question like a wall between us.

Is the world going to end next week or not?

"Well, what do you think?" I asked again, this time in a
desperate whisper, which made it even worse.

He moved into the biggest silence I have ever heard.
Simply wrapped himself up in it.

My traitor tongue went clattering along on its own,
disconnected from my brain or any shred of sense I had
left. "Because," I said, "if you don't believe that, why are
you here?" I needed him to be a true Believer, to shore up
my own greasy faith.

He stared at me for a long time, as if memorizing my face so he could dodge me for the rest of our lives, making me glad that there was only a week left before Armageddon.

Then he drew in a breath and said, "Because my dad is here. And he's such a dope, somebody has to take care of him."

And my heart, which had been made into an ice pack at his silence, melted. Of course he—Jed!—would do that. Take care of his dad. See him through to the End of the World.

Of course.

Which made no sense when I tried to parse it like a sentence later. Much later. A lifetime later. Jed was one of the Believers, yet he wasn't here because he believed. Which should have changed the numbers on the Believer board but didn't.

Still, at the moment it seemed absolutely the most wonderful reason in the world for him to be here. It even helped kick-start my own faltering soul.

"I understand," I whispered. Because I did. And suddenly I understood something else, too. "I am here—sort of—for the same reason. For my mom, if not for God."

If ... not ... for ... God.

I couldn't believe I'd said that. I could feel that rash of unbelief prickling again on the back of my neck, spreading up over my cheeks, down over my shoulders. I prayed for help. A lightning strike or a command from the sky would do.

But the only voice I heard was Jed's.

"I wish *I* understood," he said, which made me love him the more.

" 'Christ will explain each separate anguish in the fair schoolroom of the sky,' " I quoted.

"What?"

"It's Emily Dickinson."

He looked at me blankly.

"The poet," I said.

"I *know* Emily Dickinson's a poet. You can't go to school in Massachusetts and not know. Emily D. and Robert Frost. Stopping by the snowy woods every winter and the admiring bogs every spring. But what does *she* have to do with this place?"

"Everything," I said, all at once miserable. Maybe what I should have said was, *Nothing*. Or maybe I should have just *said* nothing. Because nothing prepared me for what came next.

"Did you know," Jed said suddenly, "that Beelson has this plan about the men and the . . ." He hesitated for a moment and stared at me as if reading my face.

"About the men and the what?" I asked.

He looked down at his feet. His voice got really low. "Eves," he said. "Adams and Eves."

"You don't mean—"

"It's true." He was still looking down at his feet. "Honest to God, it's true."

What, I thought fervently, *does God have to do with it?* And then I thought about the men in the camp. Old men. With big bellies. Or little hair. Old enough to be my—

"You're making this up," I told him fiercely.

He looked up at me and said just as fiercely back, "How else will the world's population be renewed afterward?"

"So you *do* believe the world is going to end?" Though it no longer seemed to matter.

"No way," he said. "But *if* it happens..." He stopped, sighed. "If..."

We had another one of those long silences, but my mind went racing on. I was thinking that if Dad knew what Reverend Beelson wanted from me, from the girls, to be ... Eves ... for the men, he'd be upmountain in a flash. Or if Mom knew, we'd be down. Surely dying in flames was preferable. Surely God didn't want such a thing to be true. I took a deep breath. *God*... I prayed.

And then I realized that I had nothing more to say to Him.

Nothing at all.

"Listen," Jed said, changing the subject, for which I was eternally grateful. "It's just about midnight. If you'll keep watch down a ways, I'll bring the laptop out. It's hard getting good reception in the cave. I only dare listen to the news as long as no one knows I've got the laptop here."

"The news?"

"Well, what did you *think* I was doing?" he asked.

It took me a moment to remember what I had thought. "I heard ... music," I said slowly. "I thought you came up here to listen..."

"I *promised*," he answered witheringly. "I'd hardly break that promise for rock and roll. That was just a piece on some world-beat band on NPR. They're called Boiled in Lead. Appropriate for the world's end, don't you think?"

He was so sarcastic all of a sudden, I scooched away from him and almost slid down the rocky scree. Then I caught myself and gave myself a mental scolding. Jed wasn't angry with me. It was everything down the mountain that remark was aimed at. Down the mountain from where we were sitting.

"I'll watch," I said. "I'll keep watch all the night, if you need me to."

"Is that more Emily Dickinson?" Jed asked, grinning.

"Just more Marina," I answered. Then I stood up and walked a little way down the mountain to stand a silent sentinel while he listened to the midnight news.

28

Jed

I sat on the rocky slope, fiddling with the laptop's radio function and thinking about Marina. She was kind of weird.

But then, I suppose all girls are, when you get right down to it. Believers or not.

Also, she wasn't what you'd call pretty. No, I take that back. She was very pretty, just not in the typical way. The things that really got to me were her eyes, which were big and soft as a deer's. Her eyes, and her hair, and the fact that she seemed so sincere and so fragile that I wanted to say, *Stay with me. I'll protect you.*

Except I figured that if I did she would just laugh.

Which shows you that I'm probably about as dumb about women as my father.

Anyway, Marina went down the trail to stand guard— or keep watch, as she preferred to say—while I tried to pick up a news broadcast. I could hear her singing softly to herself as she went, her voice clear in the night air. It made me reluctant to turn the radio function back on. I wanted to listen to her instead.

Telling myself not to get soppy, I turned back to my job. The next problem was what station to try for. The NPR channel I had pulled in just before Marina showed up was Boston based. They always had a lot of news, but I was afraid this story might still be too local for a big-city station.

Dave and Big Jim were another possibility, but the way they handled the news was spotty at best, and unless they were using the story to set up some kind of joke, it might not make their show tonight.

If I had really been thinking, I would have tried to do a wireless Internet connection with the laptop's cell-phone function. Or maybe not, since I was trying to preserve the battery and the phone's a real power drainer.

Finally I remembered the golden-oldies station my great-grandmother always used to listen to. She lived in Springfield, which was close enough to make us a local story. And the station's local news always seemed to go on forever. I mean, it covered *everything*.

I knew the call number, because I used to have to tune it in for Gramma when we visited, and I found the station with no problem. I almost wished I hadn't, since the first story was so scary it almost made me drop the laptop. Some of the atomic bombs that had disappeared when the old Soviet Union broke up had resurfaced. A terrorist group had them and was threatening to set them off in world capitals before the end of the month. The FBI was dismissing it as a hoax. Even so, the idea sent a chill sweeping through me. Not because I was afraid of the bombs. Or not entirely.

The chill came because the news made me wonder if

Reverend Beelson was right after all. It sure sounded like an end-of-the-world scenario. I shivered, imagining the nuclear fire that we could rain down on the earth. God didn't need to lift a finger. We could do the frying all by ourselves.

The newscaster was already moving on to other items, as if his attention span was too short to stay on any one subject—even the possible end of the world—for more than about thirty seconds.

Even so, I had chosen my station well. After three or four minutes of national news, I heard, "Lots of controversy on a western Mass. issue tonight. Seems the so-called Believers camping up on Mount Weeupcut to wait for the end of the world have closed their doors and aren't accepting any new members into their club. That's not sitting well with a number of people who've suddenly decided that they believe, too, and want to get up there to avoid being—as one of them put it—'fried with the rest of you sinners.' Complicating the situation is the fact that another group also wants to get in—a handful of parents, divorced or separated, whose former spouses have taken their children to the camp. Here's what one of them had to say earlier tonight."

He played part of an interview. I recognized the voice of the guy he was talking with immediately—it was the red-faced guy in the 4-Runner.

"My daughter, Tiffani, is up on Mount Weeupcut. I want to see her, and this nut Beelson doesn't have any right to keep me out. We've got lawyers on this, and the police, too." Then his voice got real dark, and he said, "And if that doesn't do any good, there are other ways to deal with this matter."

152

And that was it. The restless announcer moved on to another story.

Sometimes I want to whack those guys on the head and say, *Give us the details!*

I turned off the laptop and headed down to where Marina was waiting. She jumped a little when she heard me coming, but didn't say anything until I was standing beside her.

"Any luck?" she whispered.

"Bad luck," I replied, and began to tell her what I had heard, starting with the interview with the guy who wanted to get up here to get his kids. I figured I would save the bomb thing for last.

As I spoke Marina's eyes got wider, and a weird look—half sorrow, half relief—twisted her face.

29

Marina

The man who was interviewed—for a moment I thought it had to be my dad. But Jed shook his head. "The guy said his daughter was named Tiffani. Isn't she the one..."

I sighed. "With an *i*!" We both laughed. I think I was relieved—and yet not relieved. I didn't want Dad charging up here if there were guns around. I could just imagine him blazing back with his turkey-hunting rifle and starting a real Armageddon on his own. Yet at the same time I wondered why he didn't care enough to try. And while I was no longer certain the world was going to end, I wanted Dad to *want* to be saved with us. Or to save us. Which was the same thing, really.

Suddenly all the hurt I had felt about Dad, which I must have been holding in for days—for weeks, even— came up, and I made a peculiar sound that was just me keeping myself from crying.

Jed got that *oh-my-gawd* look that boys get when girls go *splah* on them, and gulped hard. I could see his Adam's apple bobbing twice in his throat.

Adams, I remembered. *Eves*, I thought. I swallowed

down any sign of tears and said, "You have to let him know."

"Him?"

God, I thought, already knew. My dad didn't seem to care. "Reverend Beelson," I said. "Jed, you have to tell him about the news. About the lawyers and the police and the mothers and fathers coming to get their kids. With the guns and things, it could get nasty."

He turned away before I could read the look on his face. "Then he'd know I broke my promise."

"And with all this craziness going on ... you care about that?" I whispered to his back.

He whipped around, facing me. "Shouldn't I? Shouldn't I care what Beelson thinks?"

"God and you already know," I pointed out sensibly.

"*God*," he said. He didn't say it with admiration. Then he added, "You know it, too." He put his head to one side and looked at me calculatingly. "I suppose if I don't tell Beelson, you will."

I thought about that. I thought about it a long time. Someone had to tell Reverend Beelson, because it was imperative that he know about the danger. There were little kids on the mountain, after all. But—and this I knew with sudden and absolute certainty—that someone was not going to be me.

"No," I said, slowly shaking my head. "I'm not going to say anything. *You* are. And I will go with you, all the way if you need me to."

The look he gave me this time was really odd. Like he had thought me one kind of girl and suddenly found out I was something else: an alien from outer space, maybe.

Or a vampire.

155

Or—a boy!

Then he blurted out, "OK. OK. You're right. I'm the one. But ..." And he hesitated.

"But what?"

He gulped and drew himself up, as if by making himself taller he could say the next thing, the hard thing, because it wasn't a guy thing to say. "I *would* like it if you came along."

So that's why we went back down the mountain to Cut House together, close but not touching. Side by side, but each—somehow—alone.

The path was harder going down than coming up, and we both stumbled frequently and slid on the loose scree. Once I even went down on my bottom, which hurt like stink, but I didn't cry. I bit my lip, but I made sure I didn't moan. Jed reached down and pulled me up, and didn't let go of my hand for the longest time.

Little pebbles underfoot slid away from us, pattering down the hillside in a cascade of sound. I bet we made enough noise for an invasion force, and yet we didn't care.

We were like a righteous army.

We felt, somehow, all-powerful.

And I—I felt Certain, which felt great.

Then the lights of Cut House were ahead of us, and Jed dropped my hand and began to walk ahead of me, faster and faster.

"Wait," I called in a harsh whisper. "I'll go in with you."

But I knew already from the speed he'd traveled the last hundred feet that he had to go the rest of the way alone.

156

30

Jed

As Marina and I headed down the mountain a jumble of thoughts ran through my brain, including:

a. I'm glad she's with me;

b. She's a major pain in the butt;

c. What would happen if I tried to hold her hand?

d. Reverend Beelson really does need to know what's going on down below;

and

e. Reverend Beelson's problems are none of my business, and I don't need to tell him a damn thing.

To tell you the truth, I seriously considered ditching Marina when we got to Cut House and just making a run for it.

The problem was, if I did that I wouldn't be able to talk to her again. Ever. And even though she was a major pain in the butt, I *did* want to talk to her again. Like I said, something about her got to me. Only, it wasn't the fragility I thought I had seen before. (She sure hadn't been all that fragile when she decided I had to go talk to Beelson!) It

157

was something else, something it took me a while to find the word for. It was her *intensity*. Things seemed to mean more to Marina than they did to most people. As I came to find out, that intensity meant that she hurt more than most people, suffered more when things went wrong. But it also meant that she enjoyed things more, laughed harder, was more *alive* than anyone I had ever met. I hadn't experienced all that yet, of course. Maybe I just saw it in her eyes.

We had to cross a tricky place, a steep slope where the pebbles rolled out from beneath your feet. Marina slipped, and I reached down to help her up.

Her hand felt good in mine, small and warm and firm, and once she was on her feet, I didn't let go. She didn't try to take her hand back, either. So we continued on, hand in hand. She moved closer to me. I held her hand more tightly.

As we came farther down the mountain the lights from Cut House's windows began to show through the trees. When I saw them I felt my stomach sink. Trying to figure out why, I realized I had been hoping it would be too late to visit Beelson tonight, and that I could put the whole thing off until morning.

With no way to escape, I began to think of what I should say. As I did, as I tried to imagine the scene, I suddenly realized how brave it had been of Marina to offer to come in with me. Doing so would have meant admitting she had been out of her tent when she shouldn't have been.

Up on the mountain.

With a boy.

More specifically, a boy her mother didn't approve of.

From what I had seen of Mrs. Marlow, those were sins for which Marina would pay dearly.

Which was why I ditched her about a hundred yards from Cut House. Not so I could run away from facing Beelson, which I had briefly considered.

Just so that she wouldn't have to come in with me.

I had almost made it to the main entrance when I suddenly realized I was still carrying the laptop. I turned, sprinted back, and pressed it into Marina's hands.

"Take this," I whispered urgently. "Hide it for me!"

"But I can't—"

"Please!" I hissed.

She stared into my eyes with a look that I feared might be going straight through my head and coming out the other side. "All right," she said at last. "For you."

"Thanks. Wish me luck!"

Then I kissed her on the cheek. Before she could protest, I was racing back toward Cut House.

I entered the building quietly—not sneaking, really. Just not wanting to bring attention to myself right away.

The stone fireplace held a roaring blaze, and the air smelled a little smoky, as if the chimney was not drawing as well as it should. But at least the building was nice and warm. It felt good after the mountain coldness.

The room was set up differently than for Services; the pulpit and folding chairs had been put away, the stuffed furniture brought back from against the walls. But the biggest difference was the rifles leaning against the far wall.

159

Near the fireplace stood two wooden tables, set end to end. Thirteen men were gathered around the tables. Several of them I knew to be Angels; I figured the rest were, too. All except one. The thirteenth man, sitting at the head of the table, was Reverend Beelson himself.

"Frankly, it's getting worse fast," said one of the Angels, as I closed the door softly behind me. "We must have had twenty cars come up today, and some—"

He broke off when Reverend Beelson put a hand on his arm. The Reverend stood and turned toward me. "What is it, Jed?"

My face got hot. "I need to talk to you," I said, in a voice that came out smaller than I intended.

Reverend Beelson didn't say anything for a moment, just furrowed his brow a bit, as if trying to figure out what to do about me. Finally he turned to the men. "I'll be back in a few minutes. See if you can finish working out the schedule for the sentries while I'm gone."

He left the table and walked toward me.

Geez, but I wanted to run. I don't know why, really. He didn't look angry. It's just that he was so powerful. I don't mean physically, though he really was a big guy. I just mean...powerful; the way Marina was intense. It sort of surrounded him, and you could feel it when he came toward you.

"Let's go in here," he said, resting his hand on my shoulder and directing me toward a smaller room that opened off to the right. When I saw the rumpled cot, I realized that this must be where he slept. No mere tent for the big guy. Still, it was hardly the lap of luxury.

The room also had a small window, two stiff wooden

160

chairs, a desk littered with papers, and a closet. Beelson swung the closet door shut as we came in, but not fast enough to keep me from seeing the semiautomatics inside. They made the guns out in the main room look like pea-shooters.

He gestured to one of the wooden chairs and pulled the other over to face it.

"What's bothering you, Jed?" he asked, focusing on me as if I were the only person in the world, as if he didn't have a camp to worry about, and the end of the world creeping up behind him.

I swallowed and looked down. "I broke my promise," I whispered, annoyed with myself for not being able to face him.

Reverend Beelson took a deep breath, then let it out in a sigh. "'For all have sinned and come short of the Glory of God,'" he said sorrowfully.

I looked up, smiling. "Romans. Chapter three, verse twenty-three."

It was luck, really, one of the three Bible verses I knew by heart from sixth-grade Sunday school. But I think it impressed him.

"It was good of you to confess," he said. "It must have been weighing heavily on your soul to bring you here at this time of night."

"To be honest, sir, I came because——"

I stopped myself in time to avoid saying, *because Marina talked me into it*. I didn't want to drag her into his. After a second I said, "I came because I'm worried."

"It's all right, Jed. God will forgive you. And you're safe here on the mountain."

"Safety is what I'm worried about," I said. "And it's why I broke my promise. I went up on the mountain to listen to the news because of something I saw down at the gates this morning."

Damn! I had only intended to confess about the laptop. Here I was blurting out that I had been skipping work detail, too. With a mouth like mine, who needs enemies?

Beelson didn't say anything, though, just nodded and waited for me to go on.

"From what I heard, it looks like there's going to be a lot of people trying to get up here, soon. And not just people who've decided they don't want to be fried."

He shook his head slightly. "I don't like that phrase, Jed. It's disrespectful."

I started to say something else disrespectful, but then realized I had never heard Beelson himself use the term. So I bit the words back and just said, "Whatever. The point is, some people who have kids in the camp are getting pretty upset because they can't get in to see them."

"When a family divides, tragedy always follows," he murmured.

"Well, sometimes it just happens!" I said sharply.

Without missing a beat he said, "Your mother didn't leave because of anything you did, Jed."

Though his words were soft, I snapped my head back as if he had slapped me. My questions about what he knew about my family and how he knew it dissolved in a single burning thought: *What a big mouth my father has!*

Hard on its heels came another thought, equally disturbing: *How does Beelson know I sometimes worry that it was my fault, that my mother left because of something I did?* That was

162

nothing I had ever told my father. It was something I kept hidden, deep and far inside.

I stood up, confused and angry. "Look, these people are talking about police and lawyers and who knows what all. I just thought I should warn you that there might be some real trouble coming. Sorry I bothered you."

I turned to leave, but Reverend Beelson reached out and took my hand. "You did right to come, Jed," he said softly. "I've been expecting this. Fearing it."

To my astonishment, I saw tears well up in his eyes.

He tightened his grip on my hand. Closing his eyes, which caused the tears to leak out and roll down his cheeks, he whispered, "Pray with me, will you, Jed? Pray with me, because I'm going to need all the help I can get to face the tests that are coming."

He dropped to his knees, dragging me with him.

No, that's not true.

And I swore I would make this the truth.

Though Reverend Beelson's hand was heavy on my arm, it was his need that pulled me down beside him, prompted me to kneel and pray, despite how foolish I felt.

It probably wasn't a very satisfactory prayer, from his point of view. I didn't address it to God, or Jesus, but sort of to the universe at large.

Help him, I prayed. *Help this man.*

Because I had seen something in his eyes, something I don't think he had ever showed anyone else in that camp.

He was surrounded by his Believers. They were his flock, and he loved them. But every one of them was counting on him for guidance, advice, and protection. Counting on him to make the right decisions.

Counting on him to save them.

Him and God, of course.

But God wasn't talking at the moment.

Which may have explained the fear and loneliness I had seen in Reverend Beelson's eyes.

164

Reverend Raymond Beelson
to the Believers on Mount Weeupcut
July 22, A.D. 2000

"THE TIME OF TESTING"

And so now the Day of Doom draws near. The Fires
of the Apocalypse are being kindled, and the Rain of
Terror is about to fall.

This, my children, is the time of greatest danger, the
time when we will be most sorely tested. Already the
Unbelievers and the Scoffers are beginning to doubt their
doubting, to wonder if we are right. And in their fear
these Last-Minute Christers now seek the safety of our
camp.

They cannot be allowed in. They *must* not be allowed
in. The Word of the Lord is clear. He has called for one
hundred and forty-four Believers to come to this
mountaintop.

Not one less.

And not one more!

As the End draws near, we shall be besieged.

We shall be set upon.

We must defend this place, which is our home and

our refuge, the place of safety to which the Lord has led us.

We must defend our Family.

The End and the Beginning, the Omega and the Alpha, are racing toward us. And in times to come your Lord will ask you where you stood on the day that they arrived.

What will you tell Him? Will you say you let man's law, which has been made corrupt and sinful, be placed ahead of His Great Truth?

Or will you be able to say that you fought with every ounce of strength you have for what you know to be right?

31

Marina

Isn't it odd how elastic time can be? Like a rubber band that is stretched, collapses, then is stretched again. When we came up the mountain to wait for the End of the World, we knew we had two weeks. Fourteen days. Three hundred and thirty-six hours. Twenty thousand, one hundred and sixty minutes. I worked it out by hand the first day we were here. No calculators were allowed, of course.

That feels like a lot of time when you look at the minutes. It feels like no time at all when you think about the weeks.

When we first arrived, one of the Sistern had hung a cardboard clock with a movable hour hand on the lectern in Temple. There were fourteen hours marked on the clock instead of twelve, to count down the fourteen days left till the Apocalypse. So whenever Reverend Beelson preached Service, I couldn't help but stare at the numbers, because we always sat right in front. Watching them mark off the time we were supposed to have left.

And now more than a week was gone—nine of those days—and what did I have? A boy who had kissed me once and a family squabbling all the time. I had begun the week knowing no one but my family and ended it involved with hiding a computer for a boy I hardly knew. An odd progression, when you think about it.

Odder still, since math had never been my best subject in school, was that I was suddenly obsessed with numbers. Surrounded by, swamped by, overwhelmed by them. The number of Believers. The numbers of the hymns. The number of days till Armageddon.

Numbers!

I was so tired of numbers.

Still, even though I no longer really believed we Believers were going to rule a ruined world, I couldn't stop counting. It was as if by knowing exactly how much time was left till July 27, I had some control over my life.

I didn't need Reverend Beelson or anyone else to preach about the awful fires in Revelations for me to know that some kind of Armageddon was at hand. All I had to do was look at what was happening to my brothers.

Martin, like Leo, was having problems with the food. He complained all the time about it, while Leo just wouldn't eat. After the first few days, when the fresh food had run out and we had only the canned stuff, Martin never sat at a meal without whining.

"Can't we order pizza?" he had asked Mom one day. Her only answer had been the Look.

To be honest, the food we were getting wasn't any worse than school cafeteria food. And as long as we could get to the first sitting on time, it was also hot. There were lots of three-bean salads, too, which I have always been

168

partial to. But even I had grown tired of them. I suspected whoever had done the buying had gotten a great bargain on cans of green beans, pintos, and limas.

On the morning after my midnight with Jed, however, Martin did more than complain. He let out an awful scream. He hadn't done that sort of thing in years. It was an attention getter, all right, and so loud, Mom's face turned beet red. *Fresh beets would be nice for a change,* I thought irrelevantly, and I don't even much like them.

Mom slapped Martin's face twice, the sound as sharp as gunshots, and he stopped screaming.

Two of the Sistern jumped up and took hold of them both, for a kind of time-out. Martin went quiet at once, almost suffocated between the two big women. Meanwhile Reverend Beelson came over to pray with them. Mom looked at Reverend Beelson's face while he prayed, and slowly the anger drained from her cheeks. He patted her hand and she fluttered her eyelids up at him, and then down.

And I realized suddenly, horribly, how young my mom was still.

Whose Eve are you going to be? I thought, and then bit my lip to keep from asking the question aloud.

Jerold and Jordan were sitting right by Martin, looking, as usual, like tattooed savages. Scratched head to toe from running through the brambles, they hadn't actually taken a bath in days.

They'd been acting like savages the entire week, too, hooting and hollering and often playing a game they made up called frying-the-farm, where they stood on the side of one of the cliffs and used sticks as guns to shoot down the mountainside at imaginary people, shouting, "You're fried!" and "You're toast!"

The minute Mom slapped Martin, they started chanting, "You're fried! You're toast!" at him till one of the Angels had to come and take them outside.

Grahame sat through the scene without comment, which was unlike him. But of all my brothers, I think he was the one who was changing the most. For example, two days before he had begged Mom to take him down the mountain to get more books because he'd read all the ones he'd brought with him. And when Mom wouldn't let him go, he'd tossed all his books out of the tent before bedtime.

It must have begun raining sometime later that night. By morning the rain was heavy and steady, and Grahame's books were mostly unreadable. I offered to lend him some of mine, which he resisted loudly, since he prefers science books and I prefer poetry. Instead he took Mom's Bible and began reading it with the intensity he used to reserve for the encyclopedia. He seemed especially fascinated by Revelations.

"Did you know," he said, when Mom was calm again and the two Lady Angels were back in their seats and Reverend Beelson was gone from the dining tent, "did you know that there are seven seals and seven angels and seven trumpets and——"

And that's when I lost it big time.

"No more numbers!" I shouted, surprising us all. I got up and stomped from our table in a fury.

Zondra and Tiffani were laughing at me as I passed

their table, and still in the same murderous state, I hissed at them, "Beelson means us to be Eves, you know. Eves! For all these old Adams! So what do you two think of that?"

And Zondra replied, "Pick of the litter, I guess," while Tiffani smirked.

What could I do but walk on, astonished, frightened, and angry in equal measure.

32

Jed

I was hoping to get my laptop back from Marina before too many days went by. But it meant finding a time when I could be alone with her at her tent, which wasn't easy.

Saturday, there was never a moment that seemed right. But Sunday afternoon, I thought I finally had my chance. Alex and I had been walking the fence line, to make sure it was secure, when I slipped and fell into one of the little streams we had to cross. I didn't hurt myself, but my pants were soaked, and Alex sent me back to change.

I decided to swing past Marina's tent on the way. I didn't really expect to find her, since she would probably be out on some work detail. But I also figured it couldn't hurt to check, since I knew she sometimes came back there to baby-sit her little brother, Leo.

When I got to the tent, I could hear someone rustling around inside. Delighted by my good luck, I walked quietly to the front of it, scratched on the flap, and hissed, "Hey, Marina. It's me. Jed."

I'm glad I didn't know Marina well enough to be any more familiar than that. God knows what would have happened if I had said something like, "Hey, Marina, get your sweet butt out here."

As it was, the tent flap swung open and I found myself staring into the blazing eyes of Marina's mother. The look she gave me was terrifying, and for a moment I almost wondered if the woman was channeling the spirit of Medusa. I actually felt as if my feet had turned to stone. Narrowing her eyes, she snapped, "What are you doing here, devil-boy?"

You would have thought I was Satan himself, come to offer her a cookie. I came close to popping off at her, but managed to hold my tongue for Marina's sake. Trying to sound polite and reasonable, I said, "I wanted to talk to Marina for a second."

"Well, you can't. Not now. Not ever. She doesn't talk to your type."

Obviously I knew better than that. But I decided this wasn't the moment to say so.

Mrs. Marlow narrowed her eyes and looked at me more closely. "What are you doing on the mountain anyway, boy? You're no Believer, I can see that. Not with that hair."

I wanted to ask what my hair had to do with what I believed. I would have, too, if not for the fact that I was momentarily bright enough to realize that getting Marina's mom cheesed off wasn't going to do anything to help me get the laptop back, and in fact might make it real hard for me to ever see Marina again at all.

So I just looked her right in the eyes and said in the most pleasant, sincere voice I could manage, "God bless you, ma'am."

Then I walked away.

I was glad my tongue didn't turn to stone in my mouth, since I didn't actually care if God blessed her or used her to clean His teeth. But I figured saying the blessing as sincerely as I was able ought to confuse the daylights out of her.

I changed my pants and went back to work, only by that time Alex had already finished walking the perimeter.

So I got put on a different job.

Which is how I ended up having a conversation with Reverend Beelson's firstborn son.

33

Marina

Five days before Armageddon—Sunday on the world's calendar—Jed came to our tent to claim his laptop.

I wasn't there—I was on my way to the day care to pick up Leo—but Mom was.

When she saw me later that day, she pulled me aside. Her hand was still hot from dishwater, and it felt like a brand on my wrist.

"That boy, that Devil's child, with his little pigtail and his sneer, was at our tent" was how she began. "I've seen him look at you in Temple. I've watched him watch you when you walk."

"But, Mom—" I tried to stop the flow.

She held me fast. "He asked for you, but I wouldn't tell him where you were. We have five days till the world is swept clean of sin, Marina. Don't let that boy sully you."

Sully . . . What a silly, old-fashioned word. I almost laughed. But she was serious. Her hand was like a vise around my wrist.

"He didn't *sully* me," I said. (Though he had kissed me on the cheek. I could still feel the mark of it. But I doubted there was any way she could see that.) I tried to pull away. "Mom, please . . ."

She didn't let me go, and the flood of angry words from her mouth was like a river—wild, rushing, swollen over its banks.

"He is an Unbeliever, put on the mountain to try us. Reverend Beelson says there are those who are Traps for the Unwary. Even among us, he says, there will be Those who are not yet Whole."

It was the most she had said to me in days.

I stared at her in disbelief. Jed may have looked a little . . . punk for her. And I could understand why she reacted so badly to the rattail. There'd been a group who called themselves Satan worshipers in Springfield last year, and they all wore ratty pigtails. But they also had tattoos of broken crosses on their foreheads, and skull earrings, and black lipstick—both the men and the women. Jed wasn't anything like that.

It was so horribly unjust. And whatever else Mom was, she was never unjust. Or at least the old Mom, from downmountain, was never unjust. But this Mom was more Believer than mother, so I put it in terms I thought even she would understand.

"Maybe he's to be my Adam," I said.

She stared at me and let go. "What do you mean?"

"You know. Adam and Eve. That's what Reverend Beelson says."

"What . . . what filth are you talking?" She raised her hand as if to slap me, and I suddenly remembered the gunshot sound when she had slapped Martin at breakfast.

"I'm saying what everyone else knows. That there are

only so many girls and young women, and we are to be chosen as the new Eves. To populate the world anew."

The slap landed on my right cheek. The sound of it nearly deafened me.

I forced myself to smile through the pain of it.

"Mom," I said, "I'll turn the other cheek if it will help you understand. I don't want to be anyone's Eve. Not now. Not when I am sixteen. Or even eighteen. I'm not ready to populate any world—mine, yours, or God's own. Why can't you, of all people, understand that?"

And that's when I began to cry silently.

Not for the slap, though it still hurt.

Not for the betrayal of my new feelings for Jed.

But for my mother, who had not wanted me to be born at all, who had had me because my father wanted me, who now did not know what to do with me, even though she believed the world was going to start all over again, giving us all a fresh start.

She didn't slap me again, but she didn't make a move to hold me while I cried.

And that's when I knew she wasn't my mother anymore.

We probably glared at each other through my scrim of tears for a minute. It felt like hours.

And then a sound behind me made us both shake ourselves back into the real world.

"Sister Myrna," said Mrs. Parker, her chins wobbling as she spoke, "there is something really wrong with your child." She was holding Leo's hand and dragging him toward us.

Leo looked pale, embarrassed, and exhausted at the same time. He was whimpering as they walked. Snaking down one leg, from under his tan shorts, was a long brown line.

Leo was three and he hadn't messed his pants in ages.

Mom just stood there, staring, but I squatted down and pulled him toward me.

"Oh, you poor sweetie," I said as I gathered his shivering, sweaty body into my arms. "Let's go and get you clean."

34

Jed

My new assignment was unloading the supply truck, something I had done plenty of times before.

"You'll work with L.A. here," said Hank, who was in charge of the duty roster that day.

It took me a minute to recognize the guy he pointed to as the same guy whose arrival had been the signal for the camp to close. He had been cleaned up considerably since that time. His beard, so wild and shaggy when he'd shown up, had been trimmed close to his jaw. His hair, now clean, was pulled back in a ponytail. He was wearing an old pink sweatshirt, inside-out, with the sleeves cut off and the neck cut low; from the look of his arms, he worked out. Or maybe just worked. It was kind of amazing that there had been such a good-looking guy hidden under all that hair and dirt.

"They call me L.A. because I came in from Los Angeles," he said, as if he didn't think the name was very smart.

"That must make me S.O.B.," I replied. When he looked puzzled I smiled and said, "Suburb of Boston."

His face split into a wide grin, as if he was genuinely amused. "Well come on, Suburb. Let's get busy. We've got a lot of food to unload here."

I looked in the truck. It was filled with twenty-pound bags of rice.

"That's enough to feed an army!" I groaned.

"Depends on the size of the army," he replied, scrambling into the bed of the truck. "Big-enough army could polish that off in a day. Our little army is going to have to eat for a year. Here, catch!"

And with that he tossed me a bag of rice.

I caught it, trying not to stagger.

We worked in silence for a half hour or so, developing a rhythm that let us move a lot of rice. My arms were aching, and my chest started to hurt from the bags that had thumped against it, so I was relieved when L.A. suggested we take a short break.

We sat side by side on the back of the truck, watching the camp, enjoying the sunshine and sweet air. After a few minutes I said, "So, is Reverend Beelson really your dad?"

L.A. shrugged. "That's what he's always told me."

I nodded. "I'm here because of my dad, too," I said, after another minute had passed.

That was meant to be an opening, but L.A. just grunted.

"People sure look up to him," I said, after another minute or so. "*Your* dad, I mean."

"Some people," said L.A. "And some people sure like to chatter. Come on, Suburb. Let's get back to work."

I sighed. As usual, I should have kept my mouth shut. Which I pretty much did for the rest of the afternoon. But that didn't stop me from thinking, which I don't ever seem to be able to shut down. And what I kept thinking was that there was something strange about L.A. Of course, I pretty much thought there was something strange about everyone here at Camp Bozo-laka-wikki-woo. But he was a different kind of strange.

I wanted to know what he was all about.

And I wanted to know what he thought of his father.

Hi.

Hi.

Great dinner.

If you like canned beans.

I was being sarcastic. And at least we're used to them.

I think if God wanted us to eat canned beans, He would have made them grow in a tin mine.

You are terrible, Jed. Really. Mom said you...um... stopped by the tent this morning.

She thinks I'm a Devil child.

It's the hair thing.

Funny, none of the pictures I ever saw of the Devil have a "hair thing."

Maybe you missed one or two. We had some in Springfield.

Maybe. Or maybe it's just my personality.

I don't think you have a devilish nature.

You don't know me very well.

I'd like to know you better, Jed.

I'd like to know *you* better, Marina.

Then you first.

Me first, what?

Tell me something about you so I can know you better. Something personal.

My mother ran off last year with a photographer from Colorado.

182

Does it still hurt?

Of course it still hurts. Why do you ask?

I think my dad has gone off with a woman from work. She has too many teeth.

Too many teeth?

Well, too many teeth showing, anyway. When does it stop hurting?

The teeth?

No—the pain of the separation.

When the world ends.

In five days?

If that's what you believe, Marina.

What do *you* believe, Jed?

Wish I knew. Maybe I'll know in five days... So, it's your turn now. Tell me something about *you*. Something personal.

I'm going to be fourteen this week.

Really? When?

July twenty-seventh.

Geez.

35

Marina

Leo had diarrhea so bad that a doctor was actually sent for from downmountain. I never found out how. He came up on Monday evening in a four-wheel-drive Bronco, with the Angels making a path for him, and no one got in their way because now the Angels were carrying really scary-looking automatic guns slung over their shoulders, which I thought awfully odd for Christian Believers.

Grahame led the doctor into the tent and said in an over-loud voice, once they were inside, "Did you know that in Revelations the angels were mighty fierce, too?"

The doctor didn't pay any attention to him; nor did Mom, who was on her knees by Leo's side, praying real hard in a continuous stream of words.

Grahame was not used to being ignored. "Did you know that gunpowder was invented by the Chinese long before there were guns?" he added. "Probably if there had been guns invented in Bible times, the angels would have carried them."

"Shut up, Grahame," I said, because suddenly angels with guns was not a comforting topic and I had my hands full enough, what with Leo's fever and Mom's praying and Martin's food problems and the twins running wild. "Just shut up."

Grahame got all sniffy and stubborn at that and wanted to tell me even more facts, until I threw him bodily out of the tent.

By this time Leo was whimpering and shivering, his hair wet with sweat, even in the cold.

The doctor took a long time with him—three-quarters of an hour, forty-five minutes, I can even tell you the number of seconds—and then he said Leo needed to be in the hospital because of dehydration.

"Dehydration?" Mom looked puzzled. "Why can't we just give him water?"

"It's not that simple, Mrs. Marlow," the doctor said, looking around the tent and shaking his head.

I could just imagine what he was thinking. We had dirty clothes piled at the feet of our sleeping bags, and Leo's were pretty ripe from his being sick. I hadn't had time to wash them yet. All of Leo's Legos were falling out of the grocery sack he had brought them up in, and some had been trampled into the dirt by the tent door. His stuffed animals were lined up on one side of the tent.

There was a makeshift bookcase made of a cardboard carton in between Solomon the whale and Mr. Muffins the black rabbit. Jed's laptop was now hidden in the bottom, with my books piled on top—hidden, but just barely.

Mom had balls of wool—she was knitting sweaters for the twins—stuck needles-down through the tarp floor, like some kind of bizarre offering to the gods of the Apocalypse.

185

We were a mess, all right. *Not the place*—I could just hear the doctor's thoughts—*for a sick kid*.

Just then Reverend Beelson came in, and he seemed to expand to fill the rest of the space in the tent.

"Reverend, the doctor says Leo has to go downmountain to the hospital," Mom said. "What should I do? I can't let him go. I can't. He's my baby. I can't lose him to the fires. Armageddon is just three days away." Her eyes were frantic, wild, and her fear began to communicate to Leo.

"Mommy," he began to cry. "Mommy! No fire! No!"

"We have two nurses up here with us, Doctor," Reverend Beelson said, his voice even, persuasive, low. "And they are Believers. Surely they can give the boy the attention he needs. He will stay in Cut House, on my own bed if necessary, and get hydrated there. We will not let him go down the mountain to be lost."

"We don't lose people in our hospital, sir," the doctor said.

"You are all lost down there, my friend. Only those who believe and have come with us to the mountain will be saved." Reverend Beelson turned and put his arm around Mom, just enveloping her, and she smiled back at him, a smile that was all innocence and joy—safely back in the fold.

"I cannot be responsible..." the doctor began.

"No, sir, you cannot," Reverend Beelson said. "Only the Lord can. And *we* trust that He *will* be, even if you do not."

The doctor promised to be back with the hydration equipment as soon as possible, after Reverend Beelson showed him Mom's insurance card with Dad's place of business and the name of our insurer on it. Though how he had that was another thing I never did find out.

So the doctor left, escorted by the Angels who didn't let him linger long up on the mountain because there were only three days till the End of the World. Reverend Beelson had told us only that morning that the "time was nigh to begin our last preparations."

Mom began to get seriously weird then. She rocked back and forth on her knees in the tent while I gathered up Leo's stuff to take over to Cut House.

"My baby's not for frying, Lord," she repeated over and over. And, "Fire, not water, Lord."

I called Grahame and Martin in to help me carry to Cut House all the things Leo might need—clean jammies, Mr. Muffin, and a bunch of books I could read to him. Then I picked Leo up in my arms. He seemed so little and so light and so scared. I whispered right in his ear as we walked, so he couldn't hear Mom behind us Praising to the sky and going on about how beautiful Reverend Beelson was, Clothed in Glory.

Reverend Beelson was clearing his own stuff out of the room that served as his bedroom when we arrived.

"Give the child to Charlie," he said, indicating his son.

I surrendered Leo reluctantly to the tattered man. He was cleaned up a lot, of course, and had trimmed his beard. But he still looked pretty tattered to me.

"I thought you said there were two nurses here."

"Charlie is a nurse."

"But he's a man," I said.

"Men can be nurses, too, Marina," Charlie said, and smiled. He had nice teeth for someone so tattered.

"Charlie was a nurse in California, in a hospice for

AIDS patients, before he burned out," Reverend Beelson said, wrinkling his nose as if he were smelling something bad.

Mom came in then, and held out her hands—not to take Leo, but as if she was looking for some kind of blessing from Reverend Beelson.

"Don't worry, Myrna," he said. "Charlie will heal your boy. He has the power."

"If I really had any power, Papa," Charlie said, shaking his head, "Everett and the other boys in the hospice would still be alive."

"You *have* the power, Charlie. You do."

"It's called modern medicine, Papa. And it's only a so-so miracle at best."

I must have looked alarmed at that, as he turned and smiled at me again. "Don't worry, little lady, your brother is going to be just fine."

I wanted to trust Reverend Beelson, but I knew with a sudden and pure conviction that I had to trust the tattered man even more. I might be on a mountaintop surrounded by Believers, waiting on a sign from God to help me Believe. But I already *believed* in modern medicine.

Just as Emily Dickinson did:

> *"Faith" is a fine invention*
> *When Gentlemen can see—*
> *But Microscopes are prudent*
> *In an Emergency.*

36

Jed

Monday evening I saw Marina sitting on the steps of Cut House, crying. I wanted like crazy to go over and talk to her, to find out what was wrong, to try to comfort her. Only, her mother was sitting next to her, which meant that my going over to see Marina would probably cause her more grief than joy.

So I asked around instead. It was Tuesday afternoon before I got someone to tell me what was going on.

"It's the boy," said Mrs. Parker, the fat lady with the multiple chins. "The littlest one, Leo. He got the back-door squirts so bad he nearly dried out and died." She shook her head, making her chins wobble. "No surprise, the way that woman takes care of her children."

Little as I liked Mrs. Marlow, that seemed like a cruel thing to say. Even so, I didn't want to get into a discussion of her child-rearing habits. So I just thanked Mrs. Parker and went on my way.

That night, after supper, I went to visit Leo—making sure Mrs. Marlow wasn't on the scene first, of course.

He looked pretty bad. I mean, he'd never actually

looked that good to begin with. Not that he wasn't cute and all. He was cute as the dickens. But he'd always had that kind of pale, big-eyed look kids get when they're feeling crappy.

He was in the side room that had been Beelson's bedroom. One skinny arm was hooked to an IV tube. His other arm was resting on his chest, and he had two fingers in his mouth, just like when I had first seen him. Only, now his nose was clean.

Standing next to him was L.A.

"What are you doing here?" I asked, somewhat surprised.

"Taking care of Leo," he answered. "I'm his nurse."

"Djed!" said Leo sleepily, taking his fingers out of his mouth. "Hi, Djed!"

"Hey, Tiger," I said, going close and ruffling his hair. "How ya doin'?"

"I'm sick," he said, making his eyes even bigger and more pathetic looking. "Very sick. Charlie is taking care of me."

"Charlie needs to pee," said L.A. softly, speaking above Leo's head so that only I could hear. "You gonna be here for a minute, Suburb?"

"Take your time," I said, hoping Mrs. Marlow wouldn't show up while he was gone.

"Thanks, kid."

I sat down next to Leo.

"Tell me a story!" he demanded.

So I did. I like telling stories. It took me a while to think of one that wouldn't get his mother all bent out of shape if she found out I'd told it to him, but finally I decided on Noah and the Ark—which seemed like a safe bet in this place.

I got so wrapped up in what I was doing I didn't even notice L.A. coming back into the room. I had Leo laughing pretty good by that time, since I was telling him some of the problems old Noah had had with the animals, adding a few details that don't actually show up in the Bible.

"You do good stories, Djed," said Leo, when I was done.

Then he stuck his fingers back in his mouth and went to sleep.

"Not bad, Suburb," said L.A., once Leo was resting easy. "Ever think about going into medicine? You've got a good bedside manner."

"I didn't think there was going to be a need for doctors in the world to come."

L.A. shrugged. "Depends on what you believe."

"What do *you* believe?" I asked, embarrassed by the urgency I could hear in my voice.

He stared at me for a minute. "I believe you do what you have to do," he said at last.

And my sister thought *I* held stuff in.

"So what prompted you to go into medicine?" I asked.

"My brother, Everett, got sick." L.A. sat down next to Leo's bed. "He caught AIDS."

"Were you able to help him?" I asked.

He looked at me for a long time, and I could see that he had his father's eyes, and some of his father's fierce power.

"I helped him die," he said, after a long silence.

"Geez," I whispered.

Neither of us moved for a long time.

"That was the last time I saw my father," he said at last. "Until four days ago, I mean."

I guess there are all kinds of ways for a person's world to end.

191

A SHORTER CONVERSATION

Hi.

Hi.

Your little brother looked pretty sick. Pretty cute and pretty sick. I visited him today.

Why did you do that?

Because I have a good bedside manner. I might even go into medicine someday.

The tattered man is taking care of him. Charlie.

The men call him L.A. Like the city.

Well, he's OK, like the state.

You're quick.

Sometimes. I think you make me quick.

Careful. You'll make me blush. Boys don't like to do that.

I'll be careful.

Promise?

Promise. See, link your two point fingers together. That means *I promise*.

"Point finger"? I haven't heard that since ... since the Thumbkin song.

Index finger, then.

I like *point* finger better.

So do it.

192

Do what?
Make the promise sign.
And promise what?
Promise ... Oh, I don't know.
Promise you'll talk to me?
Whenever I can.

Marina

37

Marina

The thing about endings is, they can begin quietly enough. That's how they sneak up on you.

Wednesday, the day before Armageddon was due to arrive, I took the sleeping bags from our tents to air them out before morning Praise Service. They were awfully ripe. Especially Leo's.

Mom had escorted Leo and the twins over to the trench first thing in the morning. Leo was still too weak from the dehydration to be off on his own with the Littlest Angels. But after thirty-six hours in Charlie's care, he was so much better he was even drinking on his own. He seemed to like Charlie a lot, and Charlie was as gentle with him as Dad used to be. That might not be what Reverend Beelson meant when he said Charlie had the power, but it worked just the same.

The twins couldn't be trusted by themselves anymore. They had what Jillian's mother called summer-camp-itis. She had laughed when she said it, but I don't think she thought it was particularly funny. Her gift for conversation was as limited and uncomfortable as her daughter's.

So Mom was riding herd on the three boys, finally acting like a mother again—but only because Reverend Beelson had instructed her to do so—which left me to get the tents cleaned up. We were all doing last-minute things like that, getting ready for Armageddon. And to make things even more difficult, everyone but the kids under ten was supposed to be fasting.

I seriously considered striking both of our tents and letting everything just bake in the sun, a tasty-looking sun, as yellow and round as a cookie.

Bake. Tasty. Cookie.

Funny how when you're fasting you tend to use a lot of food images.

It was a pretty day, not a cloud in the sky. You shouldn't get that kind of weather on the day before the World is supposed to end. You should get wind and rain, thunder and lightning. You should expect *fire and brimstone.*

A small breeze puzzled through the tent city, and I could see Jillian over where Mary and Joseph—as I called the young couple with the baby—lived. Jillian was playing with the baby while Mary hung out her clothes. The baby was waving a little fist in the air. *So,* I thought, *Jillian has found someone to make things different for her after all, even if that someone is only a couple of months old!* It made me smile.

Over on the steps of Cut House a group of the men were talking animatedly to one another. I could almost read their conversation in their hands. Tiffani and Zondra were hanging around the bottom steps. Zondra's hair was once again in its waterfall, but Tiffani had cut hers short and she kept touching the ends, as if to remind herself of what she had done. They were acting cool, but I knew they were really trying to get the men to watch them, because they were giggling in that silly way, arching their necks and poking each other.

Eves! I thought. And I didn't mean it nicely. After all, it had been Eve who had seduced Adam into eating the apple.

Apple! That sounded good.

Suddenly there was a funny revving sound, like a lot of trucks coming up the mountain. Horns blowing. Some odd shouting. All of which was difficult to sort out, since the wind had picked up and was blowing from where I was back toward the road, carrying the sound away.

But the men on the Cut House steps stopped talking and stared fixedly down the road. Then one of them pointed and said something, and they all reacted at once. As if they had practiced the move, they turned and ran up into Cut House, emerging seconds later waving rifles.

And one machine gun.

Onward, Christian soldiers, I thought uncharitably, clutching Leo's sleeping bag to my chest, my legs suddenly stone.

The men leaped down the steps and ran toward the road, shouting to Zondra and Tiffani to stay back, to hide in Cut House. Which, of course, being city girls and tough, they didn't do. They sneaked on behind the men, giggling. If they'd had flags, they would have been waving them.

Grahame had been waiting with Martin for Praise Service to begin. They always went in early to save us seats. But as soon as the action started, Grahame left to follow the girls. Curiosity has always been his best and worst feature. Martin waited by the stairs.

I saw Grahame go out of the corner of my eye. So I

dropped Leo's sleeping bag, willed my stone legs to move, and ran after him, because who else would?

I caught him halfway between Cut House and the road. Grabbing his arm, I yanked him around.

"*Where* do you think you're going?" I shouted, my voice unnaturally loud in the sudden awful silence of the camp.

"Did you know——" he started. And before he could say anything else, that silence was further ripped apart by an explosion, like the sound of a car backfiring.

Only different.

Only bigger.

38

Jed

Hank and I were on the roof of one of the sheds, hammering away and singing an off-key version of "Nearer, My God, to Thee."

Alex was standing below us, undoing a bundle of shingles. He was the first one to pick up on the fact that something was wrong. Putting up his hand, shouting to be heard over the *thwack* of our hammers, he cried, "Hold on a second!"

We stopped.

Beneath the fading echoes of our manly blows, we heard a scream.

Hank snorted. "Probably just one of those Marlow kids." He turned and hawked a wad of spit over the edge of the roof.

I felt offended on Marina's behalf. But before I could figure out what to say, we heard a distant popping, as if the echo of our hammers had somehow kept going.

"That's gunfire!" cried Hank. He slid to the edge of the roof and jumped down.

I scrambled down, too, and Alex and I hurried after him. I half expected to be told to turn back. Hell, I half *wanted* to be told to turn back. But my adrenaline was working harder than my brain, and I kept up with them, still clutching my hammer in my right hand.

We raced to the main entrance, the only real entrance, the gate across the dirt road that led to Cut House. It was considerably more formidable now than it had been when Dad and I first came to the mountain.

Others joined us on the road, and I could see that a few dozen Believers had gotten there ahead of us.

Who had fired the shots?

Who had screamed?

To my relief, I spotted Marina standing under a tree about a hundred yards from the gate. She was holding one of her brothers, who was scowling at her and struggling to get free. But she looked just fine.

At the gate itself a group of Angels, including my father, surrounded Reverend Beelson. It was still easy to see Beelson, since he was taller than any of them.

On the other side of the gate stood a line of vehicles. They were in a line because the road was too narrow for them to park side by side. I could see six or seven, including a couple of pickup trucks. I had a feeling there were more, but the road curved around out of sight.

At the front of the line was a county sheriff's car, the bubble-gum machine on top whirling and flashing its blue and red lights, which looked weird on the sunlit trees.

Off to the side stood a knot of about a dozen people holding signs that said things like WE BELIEVE! NOW LET US IN! and HEAVEN HAS ROOM ENOUGH FOR ALL! and GOD WANTS ALL BELIEVERS! Two or three of that group were on their knees, praying.

Two cops stood beside the lead car. One of them had a

bullhorn in his hand. When he spoke into it the tinny sound echoed off the mountainside.

"Reverend Beelson, this is Deputy O'Brien of the county sheriff's department. I order you to open this gate."

"And God orders me to keep it closed!" replied the Reverend, who needed no bullhorn to be heard for a hundred yards around. "God's Law is greater than man's, my friend."

"Reverend Beelson, this is county land, and I have people here who want access to it."

"We have rented the camp for two full weeks, Deputy O'Brien. Our time is not yet up."

I was impressed with how Beelson could bellow like that and still sound reasonable.

Another man came to stand beside O'Brien. He was dressed in a dark suit and had on sunglasses. He leaned over and whispered something to the deputy. O'Brien looked annoyed, but after a second he handed over the horn.

"Reverend Beelson, this is Agent Thorne of the Federal Bureau of Investigation."

Oh, geez, I thought. *Now we're really in for it.*

I was startled by the thought.

Whose side was I on, anyway?

"You have no business here, Agent Thorne," replied the Rev. "This is county land."

"I'm afraid I do, Reverend Beelson. You have been charged with abduction, which is a federal offense."

An angry murmur rose from our side of the fence.

"Baby stealers!" screamed a woman on the other side, who was standing back by a green Mazda.

"Heaven hoggers!" cried one of the men holding the signs.

Thorne waited for the hubbub to die down, then spoke into the bullhorn again. "I am here on behalf of some parents who want to visit their children and have been denied that right. We don't want to hurt anyone, and we don't want any violence. But I must insist that you let us in."

I wondered, for an instant, if *my* mother was out there, then figured the odds that she'd heard about this mess all the way out in Colorado were pretty low.

"No child is here on Heaven's Mountain without a parent," replied Beelson. "Not only an earthly parent but also God Himself, the Father of us all, who has called us here to keep us safe. No child can be taken from this place, for that would mean that child's Death by Fire. No man or woman or child can be taken from this Holy Assembly without endangering us all. There is no adding to our number, nor subtracting from it. The Last Days are upon us, Agent Thorne, and it is not your place, nor the place of any man, to change our role in that great drama."

They went back and forth like that for a while, interrupted by occasional shouts and cries from the people with the signs, but nothing got settled. I had watched enough news stories about similar situations to know that the Feds would probably try to wait us out—to starve us out. (Heh. Not much chance of that, given the food we had stockpiled.)

And what difference did it make, really? We were only a day away from Beelson's deadline, and then it would be over, and we could all go home.

Or not. Depending on who was right.

TRANSCRIPT OF A CALL

County Sheriff's Deputy Patrick O'Brien
to Police Dispatcher Caroline Burke
8:45 A.M., July 26, 2000
From police files

O'BRIEN: Hello, Caroline?

BURKE: Hey, Pat. What's up, big guy?

O'BRIEN: Nothing good. Me and Eddie are up here on the
Cut at the Believers' camp, and things are getting
sticky. Not only does Beelson have the road blocked,
these guys are armed.

BURKE: Uh-oh. How heavily?

O'BRIEN: Big time. Semiautomatics and stuff. I don't
know how serious they are, but they just fired a
bunch of warning shots to get us to back off.

BURKE: What are you going to do?

O'BRIEN: How the hell should I know? It's a real mess, I
gotta tell you. I got Beelson's goons in front of me,
armed for bear. I got half a dozen angry parents behind me demanding to be let in. I got two state cops
breathing down my neck—

BURKE: Trying to take over?

O'BRIEN: Nah, they're not bad. The one who's really
getting up my nose is this hostage specialist the FBI

sent up. See if you can get Cartwright to give Washington a call and get this guy off my case, will ya? He's a real dork. But he's not even the worst of it.

BURKE: There's more?

O'BRIEN: Yeah, get this. In addition to everything else, I got a pile of religious nuts who want to get *into* Beelson's camp because they think he's right!

BURKE: *(laughing)* Maybe you should stay there, Pat. Save your sorry butt from frying when the end comes.

O'BRIEN: Yeah, yeah, yeah.

BURKE: So do you want reinforcements?

O'BRIEN: You're not kidding. But tell them not to come all the way up yet. Road's pretty much blocked anyway. I want them close at hand if anything starts to cook, but I'm afraid if they all show up at once it may push Beelson and his crew over the edge.

BURKE: Got you. Anything else?

O'BRIEN: Yeah. Send up some coffee and doughnuts, would ya? It's gonna be a long day.

39

Marina

Grahame refused to move back, and I refused to let him get closer. I mean, there were *guns* there.

There were guns everywhere.

The police had guns.

The Angels had guns.

And I didn't doubt for a minute that some of the other people behind the gate had guns, too.

"Grahame," I whispered to him so as not to call attention to us. "We've got to get back behind the Temple."

"Did you know—" he said, turning toward me.

"The only thing I know, you stupid boy, is that we're in danger here."

"But I thought that's what the End of the World is all about," he said, his voice sensible and loud. Much too loud. "About danger. The rush of adrenaline." He sounded for a moment like a sports announcer. Then abruptly he turned back into Grahame again. "Did you know that they make a drug from animal adrenaline that can raise your blood pressure, and—"

"*You* are raising my blood pressure. *Move* it!"

"You can't make me."

"I'm in charge. And what I say goes."

"You aren't Mom."

"*Mom* isn't Mom right now."

"Well, then, where's Dad?"

At which point we were at as much of a standoff as Reverend Beelson and the police. So we continued there, with my arms wrapped tight around Grahame so he couldn't get any closer—but I couldn't move any farther away, either.

What we did was listen to everybody bargain for time.

Reverend Beelson argued that the Believers had rented the camp for two weeks in Good Faith, and had even paid in advance, which would not be up till Friday. "We have a written agreement," he said.

The policeman, a beefy man in a blue uniform that had darker blue stains under the arms, shook a finger in Beelson's direction. "You've violated that written agreement thirteen ways till Sunday," he said.

Reverend Beelson just smiled.

"For one," the policeman added, "you've ruined the land, what with erecting fences and building storage sheds. And who is going to pay for that?"

"God will provide," said Reverend Beelson.

"And if He don't?"

"Then the Believers will," Reverend Beelson answered. "You have my word on that."

The FBI man said that kidnapping charges would be filed.

The parents on the other side of the fence began screaming for blood.

And the Last-Minute Christers—which is what Reverend Beelson called those who were too late in wanting to join us—knelt by the gate and prayed. I couldn't make out their prayers, and could only guess what they were saying.

But after about half an hour of hard bargaining, they all agreed to leave us alone till morning, though some of the LMCs climbed into sleeping bags and sat down by the gate, refusing to move.

The policeman who'd been arguing with Reverend Beelson sprawled against his car, looking as if he had no intention of going anywhere, either, until we left the mountain or the World ended, whichever came first.

And just when it seemed as if things had begun to settle down at last, up the side of the road came two large vans, a blue one with CNN on the side, and a gray one marked CBS AFFILIATE.

40

Jed

It was the longest day of my life.

Maybe the longest day in the history of the world.

We tried to go about our normal business, but it's not easy to act normal when you have cops and Feds and frantic parents and wailing converts and national media all staring in at you. Besides, it was not a normal day. It was the day before Armageddon, or so we were supposed to believe.

Fortunately, some of the outside fuss calmed down when Deputy O'Brien's reinforcements showed up and helped him usher the parents to the base of the mountain. They went, though not without shouting some really horrible things as they did.

The TV crews got that on tape, of course. But it wasn't enough for them, so they stayed on, filming across the fence and trying to entice some of us into talking. Zondra and Tiffani, the matching set of dips, were only too glad to oblige, until one of the Angels finally pulled them away from the fence and sent them off to do some work.

After about three hours the reporters must have decided we weren't going to do anything else really interesting until the next day, so they turned around and left. I figured the three hours of filming would probably translate into about five seconds on the air, a brevity for which I was profoundly grateful.

The only ones still outside the fence were the Last-Minute Christers. The scary thing was that even though I had heard O'Brien say the cops were going to seal off the road, the LMCs *kept coming*—not in cars now but on foot. Some of them came right up the road. Others came sneaking through the trees. But they couldn't get into the camp itself, not with cops at the gate and the fence charged and operating at full strength.

About two o'clock a couple of county cars came back up the road and positioned themselves in front of the gate. Deputy O'Brien got out with his bullhorn again. This time his attention was all on the LMCs.

"All right, folks," he ordered. "Move back. *Move back!*"

Eventually the deputies cleared a space of about fifteen feet in front of the gate. But since there were only four of them, they couldn't keep the LMCs away from the fence itself. They lined up along the edge of it, two and three deep in places, some of them standing, some kneeling. The air was thick with their praying and weeping and shouting.

After a while a chant broke out:

> Let us in, let us in!
> To let us fry would be a sin!

How dorky can you get? Did they really believe God was going to save those of us on this side of the fence, and zap the ones on the other side, only twenty feet away?

I guess they did.

When I thought about it, I realized that was what we were supposed to believe, too.

But then, if you've read your Old Testament you really could think God might do just that, what with Sodom and Gomorrah and pillars of salt and all that stuff. And with the nuclear scare that was going on down below, maybe hysterical fear wasn't such an irrational thing to feel anyway.

Even so, it didn't help any when Zondra and Tiffani showed up again and started walking back and forth in front of the gate with a chant of their own:

> Toast! Toast! Toast! Toast!
> Gonna be a weenie roast!

Sometimes I thought that if God *was* going to fry anyone, those two should go to the head of the list.

41

Marina

There's something about going on a fast that concentrates the mind on food. I'm not a big eater normally, but by afternoon all I could think of was something to eat. Even with everything else going on.

Reverend Beelson had warned us that "The sinning mind will turn to food. You will think, *Pies*. You will think, *Oreos*. You will think, *Spaghetti*. But let the sinning mind go, my children. Fasting will allow you to liberate the angelic mind that feeds not on the gross matter of the earth but on the heavenly matter of the heart."

So I tried. And as long as I kept myself busy cleaning up our campsite, it worked. I only thought, *Wheat Thins*. Or, *Bologna*. Or, *Apples*. Or, *Pop-Tarts*. Little sins of the mind while I tried to open the angelic heart.

Grahame tried to fast, too, but he only made it till a little past three. I gave him permission—Mom being up at yet another Bible study group—to get something from the kitchen.

"But stay away from those gates!" I shouted at his back, because though they were now pretty quiet, a lot of LMCs were still camped outside the fence. I didn't want Grahame anywhere near them.

While he was gone the twins and Martin and I tried to wrestle the two baked-out tents back up. We were having a tough time of it when Jed came by.

"Hi, Marlows," he said.

The boys greeted him but I tried to look casual, not wanting to give any camp gossips ammunition, not right before Armageddon Day, anyway.

"Need help?" he asked.

"Yes. But I'm not sure you're the one to give it," I said. "I watched you and your dad try and get your tent up when you arrived. It was pretty pathetic."

"Lady, you have wounded me sore," he said, clutching his chest like an actor in a Shakespeare play. Then he smiled shyly. "I've learned a lot since then."

"In eleven days?" I asked, but I smiled back. My heart seemed to have developed a rhythm all its own.

"I'm a quick learner. And I have the calluses to prove it." He held up his hands to show me, and pointed. "See, this one is for ditch digging. And this one is for truck loading. And this one——"

"Pooh——I have those, too," I said.

"Show me."

I turned my hand over, and part of the tent fell down. Jed ignored the tent and took my hand.

"Ah, I see. Very *unladylike*!"

"*Marina!*" Martin complained. "Finish helping with the tent!"

The twins fired off sticks at Jed. "You're toast now, Jed!" they said together. And Jerold added, "French toast! That's because you looooove Marina."

French toast, I thought, suddenly starving, *would be very nice.*

211

But I took my hand away. Not because I wanted to but because if I didn't, the twins would never shut up about it. And then even Mom would find out.

"Put up or shut up," I said.

Jed grinned at me evilly.

"The tent, I mean," I said. And then when he wouldn't stop grinning, I said again, *"The tent!"* I could feel that awful blush take over my whole body.

"I'm going to like sharing the End of the World with you, Marina," Jed said.

But then the LMCs at the gate started chanting again and Jed looked over at them, a frown dragging his mouth down.

"What is it this time?" I asked.

"It looks like there are a lot more of those protesters than before. And some of them are pretty ugly customers."

"Well," I said, "the rest of us aren't so beautiful these days ourselves."

He looked over at me and took a moment before answering. It was a poet's moment. I savored it.

Then he said, "It depends on what you count as beauty, Marina."

The world could have ended at that very moment and I wouldn't have cared a bit.

42

Jed

I felt better after spending a little time with Marina and her brothers; calmer, somehow. I could sense a kind of connection growing between us, something deeper than I had experienced with any of the girls I had dated at home. Maybe because up here on the mountain we were away from surface things, and living at a different level. While in some ways the Believers' camp was too weird to be real, in other ways it felt more real than anything I had ever experienced.

After I left the Marlows I realized I'd forgotten to ask Marina for my laptop. I thought about going back to get it, but decided to wait.

Tomorrow would be soon enough.

I stopped at David and Melinda's tent to play with baby Agnes. David was off with the men somewhere, but Melinda was there, sitting on the ground, looking wide-eyed and terrified.

"We'll be safe here, won't we, Jed?" she whispered while I was trying to coax a smile out of Agnes. "Safe on the mountain." She was worrying at a strand of her hair,

213

twisting it around and around her finger, then straightening it out, then twisting it again.

"Sure, Melinda," I said. "We'll be safe."

Once night fell the camp began to get a little calmer, though the darkness didn't stop the constant chanting and praying of the LMCs outside the gate, which was getting on everyone's nerves.

The LMCs weren't the only ones praying. By this time there was a whole lot of praying going on at the top of Mount Weeupcut: people praying for the lost below, for family and friends they hadn't been able to convince to come with us; people praying to thank God that they *were* inside; and, of course, the LMCs praying to be let past the fence so they could be inside, too.

A lot of the people were praying out loud, which is how I knew what they were asking for.

We Insiders—we had had another new name for ourselves within half an hour of the arrival of the LMCs— were supposed to have a major Worship Service at eleven, when Reverend Beelson and the Lady Angels were going to pass out the White Robes in which we were to Wait for the End. (By this time, I was starting to feel like Almost Everything should be in capital letters.)

After the Service there was going to be an all-night vigil, in case the End should start before morning. ("We know the day, but not the hour," people kept saying to each other.)

The weirdness of it all was getting to me, and I considered going back to that cave where Marina and I had first really talked, just to get away from everyone. It might have

214

been pretty funny to have the Believers start counting out their precious 144 and find they were one short. What would they do then? Have a lottery and let in one of the Last-Minute Christers?

Of course, to really enjoy the joke, I'd have to be there to see it—which would make it hard to pull off. Besides, something about the idea didn't sit right with me. I still thought these people were whacked. But, dammit, I also liked a lot of them. I couldn't betray them now. Not if I wanted to be able to look them in the face once this was all over.

So at eleven o'clock I walked to Cut House with my father, and stood for one last time with the Believers.

A hundred and forty-four tall white candles lit the Great Hall. They were the only light, and our collective breath made them flicker, so that the shadows they cast danced all around the room.

At the front of the room, behind the pulpit, were stacks of cardboard boxes.

Around me were the Believers, almost vibrating with joy and terror, eagerness and sorrow, as they awaited the End.

Reverend Beelson strode to the pulpit and began to speak.

Reverend Raymond Beelson
to the Believers on Mount Weeupcut
July 26, A.D. 2000
11:00 P.M. Service

Hear, my children, the words given by the prophet in the Book of Revelations:

You have still a few names in Sardis, people who have not soiled their garments; and they shall walk with me in white, for they are worthy. He who conquers shall be clad thus in white garments, and I will not blot his name out of the book of life.

My children, we here on the mountain have conquered doubt and disbelief. It is our names that will not be blotted out of the great book, our names that will endure.

Listen again to the prophet: *Because you have kept my word of patient endurance, I will keep you from the hour of trial which is coming on the whole world.*

That trial is but hours away. Soon, soon, the whole World will know what we have long believed.

Soon, soon, they will understand.

Listen again to the prophet: *These are they who have come out of the great tribulation; they have washed their robes and made them white in the blood of the Lamb.*

We have your robes, my children, the white robes of the Believers. We have carried them here with us, one for each of us, for the one hundred and forty-four who have come to the mountain. One hundred and forty-four, no less and no more. A dozen dozen shall we save here.

Now we will don our robes of white to prepare ourselves for the Day of Fire which is to come.

Then we will weep our lamentations for those who are about to be burned, and sing our songs of Praise for our own salvation.

today for the Eve of the Promise to come.

43

Jed

Reverend Beelson was in rare form, filled with joy that
the Eve of the Promise (that was a new one) was at hand,
yet filled with compassion for those below as well. He had
those Believers on an emotional roller coaster, soaring up
one minute and down the next, Praising and Weeping, Ex-
ulting and Mourning.

Much as I tried to stay apart from it, I could feel myself
going along for the ride—not a full-fledged Believer, just a
passenger on their bus. Part of me was longing to surren-
der to their excitement. But my head just wouldn't let me.
So I held my heart hard, keeping it safe and exempt from
their foolishness.

We got to the last hymn, and while we were singing
Beelson disappeared for a minute, down the darkened hallway toward the kitchen. He came back just before the final
amen, dressed in his snow white robe. It looked so fine in
the flickering candlelight that everyone gasped.

"Now we go to await the End," he boomed in his great
voice. "Clothed in white that reflects not how pure we are,
but how pure we would be; not our goodness, but our wish

218

for goodness. Come, my children, and don your robes. Then follow me to the top of the mountain, where we will sit this starry night and wait to witness God's judgment on this sinful world."

Two of the Lady Angels came up to help him pass out the robes, which were in the boxes I had seen at the front of the room. One of those assisting was Marina's mother.

We went forward one by one, first the children, then the women, then the men, each in turn stepping up to take a robe from Reverend Beelson's own hands. And all the while the little organ was playing and the Believers were singing.

Marina was in the kids' line. She stood at the end of it, and I was able to study her face as she waited. With the candlelight on her big eyes and pale skin, she looked almost like some religious painting.

It was her own mother who handed Marina her white robe. But when Marina reached out to take it, Mrs. Marlow didn't let go right away. They stood for a long moment, both holding the robe, staring at each other. I couldn't see Marina's face then. I wondered what was going on between them.

Suddenly Mrs. Marlow let go. Marina slipped into the robe and turned to rejoin the congregation. She caught my eye as she did. The connection was like a jolt of electricity shooting between us. Then she melted into the crowd.

Next it was the women's turn.

Then the men got in line, and I was absurdly pleased that I was included in that group, rather than with the kids.

Dad was right in front of me. Just before it was our turn to get our robes he turned and hugged me. "I love you, Jed," he whispered. "I'm glad you're here with me."

His eyes were filled with tears, and in the flickering candlelight I could see the delight and sorrow warring inside him as he rejoiced that I was saved and mourned that Alice was among the Fried.

Then he got his robe, and I got mine. I shook it out and put it on.

Dad asked me to help him with his silver candle pin, which I did. Then I gave him mine. He pinned it to my collar for me, then pulled me to him and held me close again.

As he held me I heard the weeping and the Praising of the Believers. Their joyful lamentations came from a place so deep and strange that most of us don't even know it's there. It caught at something inside me and I felt myself begin to tremble, in tune at last with their fear and longing. Suddenly it was just too hard to continue clinging to my disbelief.

I remembered that starry night on the mountain, and the thing that had happened inside me, and how I had longed to feel it again. Something hard in the center of my chest began to melt, as the stone I had made of my heart surrendered at last.

What did I believe? I don't really know—though if you had asked me at that very minute, I might actually have said it was all that Reverend Beelson had set forth. What I do know is that I felt snatched out of myself, held in the grip of something bigger and stronger and finer than I had ever imagined. It was as if in putting on the robe I had put on a new skin.

I could feel tears coursing down my cheeks and I wanted to hide them, even though I knew that as far as the

Believers were concerned it was just fine to cry in this place, at this time. But some weird part of me didn't want that to be all right with them, didn't want them to know what had happened to me.

The Angels who had been guarding the front doors of Cut House were the last to come forward to get their robes. The rest of us were singing joyously as they did, singing so loud you couldn't hear anything but the sound of our voices.

That instant of vulnerability was all it took for the Last-Minute Christers to break in.

How they had gotten through the gate, how they had come across the hundred yards of open space, how they had mounted the Cut House stairs, we were never to know. But with shrieks that sliced through my newfound joy like razors of fire, they burst through the door and started trying to wrestle the robes away from the Believers.

Christ might have turned the other cheek at that moment, but the Believers weren't about to. And I could understand that, because I was as wrought up as they were. Here we stood at the Gates of the New World, and these Outsiders, these Last-Minute Christers—who had done nothing to help, hadn't waited with us, dug with us, built with us, prayed with us, weren't any part of what we had become—were trying to take it away at the final minute.

I saw a man go screaming back out the door, one of the robes clutched under his arm, while the woman he had stolen it from collapsed to the floor, sobbing.

Someone came after my robe, too, and I decked him,

lashing out with a strength and a fury that astonished me.

Then I heard Marina cry out, and I saw a woman wrestling with her, trying to tear away her robe. I vaulted over a chair, burst between two struggling people, and grabbed the woman by the hair, trying to pull her away.

The woman spun on me, shrieking about fire and vengeance, and the look on her face was terrifying. Her eyes were wild. Spit was flying from her lips.

I don't know what I would have done next, whether I could have fought with her.

I never had a chance to find out, because that's when the first shot was fired.

44

Marina

Do you know how loud a gunshot sounds in a room? Even a big two-story room like the Great Hall?

It sounds like the End of the World.

For a moment all the confusion, all the shouting, all the fights over the robes stopped. There was this awed hush, a silence so deep I thought I must have died.

And then someone screamed. A woman. The woman who had been trying to grab my robe.

As I watched, a red flower blossomed on the front of her sweater. Only, it wasn't a flower and it didn't blossom. It was a hole filling with blood. She took a deep bubbling breath and fell forward onto Jed, who held her as if they were embracing.

"Oh, my God," I whispered. It wasn't a prayer. It was pure and awful terror. I was babbling, shaking. "Jed, you didn't? Whose gun? Is she ...?" Then I stopped, because Jed had begun to lower the woman to the floor and the front of his white robe was stained red.

"Are *you* hurt?" I cried. Only then did I realize that the blood was the woman's. Only then did I notice that Jed had no gun.

For a moment I was relieved. If he didn't have a gun, he couldn't have shot the woman. But then I saw that his eyes were wild. I thought he was going to scream.

Move! I told myself. *Help him!* And after what felt like an eternity I was able to make myself go forward. I took hold of the woman's arms and together we set her down.

I know there was crying around us. I know someone was sobbing close by. But it was like the background noise of a movie where you can hear the main characters speak clearly even though there's chaos erupting all around them.

"Jed," I said. My voice was remarkably strong, I thought. It hardly wobbled at all. Lucky his name had only one syllable. "Jed."

But he didn't look at me. He was staring past me. And when I turned to see what he was staring at, I saw a man holding a pistol. Actually I saw the pistol more than I saw the man, and the pistol was pointing right at Jed.

Then I heard lots of screaming. And weeping. I heard kids whimpering. And Reverend Beelson calling out for calm.

I was still debating whether to get between Jed and the gun. I had this crazy thought that because it was to be my birthday in minutes, I had some kind of power. Surely God wouldn't kill me on my birthday. He was only interested in destroying the rest of the world!

But I didn't move, and I couldn't move, because suddenly I realized something. My birthday meant nothing to God—so why should it matter to anyone in this crowd? Especially to someone with a gun.

Which is when Jed spoke.

"Daddy," he said, "put it down." His voice was soft and

had the kind of intimate sweetness I dreamed of. "Put the gun down."

"Jeddie?" his father said to him. "I couldn't let her hurt you. I've already lost your mother and Alice. I can't lose you, too."

"I know, Daddy," Jed said. "I know." He stepped over the woman on the floor and closed the distance between them, his arms stretched out to comfort his father. Then a second and a third shot rang out.

The screaming started up again, and I seemed to be screaming the loudest of all. In between screams, I thought I heard my mother crying for help and saw the tattered man rushing over to the far corner, pushing people out of the way. I didn't know if it was a Believer or an Unbeliever he was running to help.

Three of the Angels tackled some poor teenaged boy, who seemed gangly and uncertain, pushing him up against a wall so hard I heard something break.

And then Leo began calling my name.

"Marina! I want Marina!" he wailed from somewhere near me.

Suddenly I had to move. I had no choice. I started forward so precipitously, I almost stumbled.

"Round up the kids," Jed shouted after me. "Get all of them. Get them upmountain. To the cave."

I didn't need telling. I was already looking around for the source of Leo's ongoing wail. "You get there, too!" I shouted back. And then I found Leo hiding under a folding chair and, forgetting about Jed, I picked Leo up in my arms and stroked his hair.

"It's all right," I said. "I'm going to take us away from all this."

225

He snugged his head down against my shoulder so he didn't have to see anyone, as if that made him invisible as well.

That was when I saw Mom, about ten feet away, with the rest of the adults. She was standing motionless, her white robe half torn from one shoulder. She looked at me as if she was seeing me, *really* seeing me again.

"Marina!" she cried.

"Mom!" I shouted back, and raised my hand toward her.

"Get your brothers out of here!" she cried, making a shoving motion with her hand. And then she was grabbed from behind and spun around, and disappeared behind about a dozen tumbling bodies as if they were a solid wall.

45

Jed

I am never safe from that night. It keeps bursting back on me in little pieces, shreds of memory that explode in the middle of a thought, no matter where I am, what I'm doing.

A lot of those memories are of sounds: the shouts and screams, the gunfire, the great roar of Reverend Beelson's voice trying to bring order to the chaos that had erupted from his dream.

Other memories are of smells: the smell made by guns being fired, the coppery smell of freshly spilled blood, the choking smoke of Cut House burning.

Still others are of sights, though one more than any other rises again and again in my mind and refuses to go away. That is the sight of my father's eyes when he realized what he had done, the way his face crumpled in horror and shame.

Another man might have gone on a rampage then, caught up in the carnage and bloodlust that his horrible deed had unleashed. Another man might have turned the weapon on himself. Another man might have said coldly that the woman had it coming.

227

I don't know what another man would have done. I only know about my father, who stood there, tears trembling in his eyes, hands trembling on the gun. He was looking at me as if I was the grown-up, not him, and he was hoping I wouldn't get too mad at him for having broken a window.

Only, it wasn't a window he'd broken.

"Jeddie," he whispered again, and as I moved toward him, two things happened. One—new shots rang out behind us. Two—Dad's hands uncurled and the gun fell to the floor.

I stared at the thing, repelled and yet thinking I should grab it, thinking we needed it.

That instant's hesitation was enough; someone else snatched the gun from the floor, though whether it was a Believer or an LMC I couldn't tell.

Behind me I heard Leo calling for Marina, and I realized we needed to get the little ones out of this madhouse, get them someplace safe.

"Round up the kids," I shouted to her. "All of them. Get them upmountain. To the cave."

Our eyes locked for just a second. "You get there, too!" she shouted back. I wanted to, wanted to go right that second, both to help her and to escape from this place. But I had to stay, had to take care of my father. It was the only reason I'd come to the mountain to begin with. So I just linked my fingers in our special promise sign.

Then I turned back to the woman my father had shot.

I was thinking we had to get her out of there, too; get her some medical help. I wondered where L.A. was, if he would know what to do.

Others had pressed in around us now, some trying to help the woman, some trying to seize my father, still others trying to protect him.

I quickly realized it would be impossible to drag the woman through that chaos.

Almost as quickly, I realized it wouldn't make any difference.

It was clear from the way she lay, like a broken toy, that she was already dead.

46

Marina

Finding my brothers was the easiest part. All of us kids, having gotten our robes first, were still pretty much together near the pulpit. The grown-ups, embroiled in fighting off LMCs, were on the other side.

I found Grahame, scared silent, like Leo, under a chair. Martin and the twins were huddling on the floor.

I made them get up and hold hands, which under any other circumstances they would never have done. But they clung to one another as if to ropes on a cliff.

"Stick close," I shouted, pulling Martin along with one hand while I held Leo up with the other.

I glanced around, but in the pushing, shoving, screaming crowd on the far side of the hall, I couldn't see any sign of Mom.

Behind the pulpit I spotted three more kids. Two were wild-eyed and whimpering. The third, a little blond girl about three years old, had fallen to the floor with her hands over her head. Hauling my brothers behind me, and using the pulpit to shield us from sight of the battlers, we got to them in seconds.

"Hold on!" I shouted.

"I want my dadda," the little girl cried.

I glanced around. No one was coming over to claim her. Wherever her father was, he was either too busy or too hurt to get to her.

"We'll find a place to stay till your dadda comes," I said.

Grahame pulled the little girl up. At first she hung back, till she saw that Grahame was just a kid, too. The others, both girls no more than five years old, reached without hesitation for the sleeve of Grahame's robe.

We hugged the wall, following it around to a corner, where we came upon Jillian. She'd been standing in the row ahead of me before the fighting had begun and was now slumped over sobbing. Since she was holding on to Mary's baby, I whispered, "Two more for the cave."

I pulled the kids even with me, then shoved them ahead, toward Jillian. Then I checked behind us. For the moment no one else was near. When I reached Jillian I touched her shoulder to get her attention. She didn't look up to see who it was but flinched, as if expecting a blow.

I put my mouth next to her ear. "It's me. Marina," I told her. "Come with us. I know a safe place."

She stopped crying but clutched the baby to her like a security blanket.

"Where's the baby's mother?" I asked. "Where's Mary?" But she didn't answer. Or couldn't. Or didn't know who I meant. I realized I had never learned the mother's real name.

The rhythm of the fighting seemed to have shifted away from us entirely, toward the front door, where some people were still trying to get in and more were trying to escape. It gave us a little bit of breathing room.

"Jillian," I said, "Listen to me!" Then I shouted her name again to get her attention.

She looked up, her eyes big and bright with tears behind the glasses.

"Do you 'know now many little kids there are altogether? I've been too busy with my brothers. I haven't paid attention. How many, Jillian? Please. It's important! Think. Think!"

She looked up finally, rubbing her eyes with her one free hand while the other kept the baby against her chest. "Don't," she said. "Know."

"Oh, for goodness' sakes, Jillian," I said. "Use whole sentences once in your life. We don't have time for fragglements."

She was so startled she blurted out, "Five girls in Littlest Angels, I think. And eight boys, including your brothers. And Ashlee and you and me and the Southies."

I took that to mean Zondra and Tiffani.

"And the cute boy with the ponytail."

"Rattail," I said automatically.

"How many is that?"

"Thirteen little ones," I said. "And then us." That was an awful number if you were the least bit superstitious.

"And baby Agnes," she said. "Fourteen."

I think we were both relieved.

We followed the wall again, moving forward in a tight group, and came upon Zondra.

"Let's get out of here," I said to her. "I know a safe place."

But she shook her head. "Where's Tiffani?" she said. "I can't go without T."

I looked around. Tiffani was probably close to the Angel she had a crush on, I thought. But she might be fighting by his side. *She might even*—and this thought made me tremble so suddenly and so hard Leo looked up, startled—*she might even be dead.*

"She's outside," I lied. But I guess I didn't do it convincingly, and Zondra refused to join us.

The fighting turned again and boiled toward us. Someone slid across the floor, bowling over two of the littler boys.

"Pick them up!" I screamed. "Pick them up!" I kicked at the man on the floor, but as I only had sneakers on, I don't think I did him any lasting damage.

Grahame picked up one of the boys and Martin grabbed another. We scuttled away till we found six other kids, including Ashlee, along the unbroken length of the east wall, their parents somewhere in the shadow land of the Great Hall, still brawling over robes.

"My dad said to stay here, out of the way," Ashlee said.

"We are going to go to a really safe place," I told her. "Your dad will be pleased."

"I don't know..." she began. But then a woman screamed horribly and the sound sped like a bullet toward us. Ashlee recoiled from the sound.

"Ashlee, please," said Jillian.

I think it was because of the scream, not Jillian's plea, but Ashlee put her hand in Martin's and the rest fell quickly, trustingly in line.

Then the tumble of the crowd shifted toward us again

233

and we had to dodge a half dozen large fighters. At one point a fat man in a leather jacket who held a big, knobby stick over my head forced me to strip off my robe. I set Leo on the floor, where he screamed uncontrollably and waved his arms at me. Tearing off my robe, I flung it at the man to keep him from grabbing me as well. As the fat man was putting on the robe, ripping it in his eagerness, Grahame went behind and kicked him in his enormous rear.

The man turned with his stick, but he never got to land a blow because someone else—I have no idea if it was a Believer or an Unbeliever—pushed him down and stomped on his hand. Grahame jumped back, tripped over Jillian's foot, and landed on the floor. But he was laughing.

"I'm a hero!" he shouted.

"Some hero!" I said. "You're on your bottom. And you could have been killed."

He got up but he was still smiling, which I could just make out in the flickering candlelight.

I picked Leo back up, and with several of the littlest kids holding on to my shirt, and Jillian and the others behind, I led us all into a dark hallway.

"This goes to the kitchen," Jillian said.

Glory be! I thought. *Another whole sentence.*

"And there's that door from the kitchen onto the back porch," I told her. "If we can find it." It was unrelievedly black in the kitchen. The candles had lit only the main room of the Temple, and I didn't want to advertise where we were.

"Is this the End of the World?" Martin asked suddenly, his voice trembling.

I thought about the woman with the red blossom of

blood on her sweater. The gangly teenager thrown against the wall and the sound of something cracking. The fat man on the floor. Jed's father with his gun.

"It is for some people," I said. "Not for us."

"Are you sure, Marina?" asked Jerold.

"Of course I'm sure," I said. "It's my birthday, after all. Who's ever wrong on their birthday?"

One of the little kids giggled, and then a second. And suddenly it was as if they had *all* taken a big gulp of laughing gas. I guessed it was hysteria, but it sure beat crying.

"Come on," I said in a steady voice, sounding much braver than I felt. "Stick close to Jillian and Grahame and Ashlee and me. We're going somewhere special to celebrate my birthday. Your parents will find us soon."

Then, more by feel than anything else, we found our way to the kitchen door and out into a night as dark as chocolate cake with candles made of flickering stars.

47

Jed

I flinched away from the dead woman, grabbed my father's arm, and headed for the front door. We hadn't gone more than ten feet before we were pulled apart by the crush of bodies.

I had never been in a mob before. It's as if you're caught in a tide or a strong current, but instead of water it's the flow and crush of bodies you have to fight against. And unlike water, these bodies were solid and willful, propelled by anger or fear, or both. I was literally swept off my feet, carried forward without being able to touch the floor.

In the chaos it took me a moment to realize what had notched everyone's fear up to another level. I had been so caught up in what was happening right in front of me that I hadn't noticed the room getting brighter. But now a whiff of acrid smoke reached my nostrils. Wrenching myself around, I saw that the 144 candles had been knocked over by the struggling crowd. Most had sputtered out or been stepped on. But some had landed in the cardboard boxes, which were starting to really blaze.

Shouts of anger gave way to screams of panic. Some of the men were trying to stomp out the fire, but I could see it was getting away from them. A few people, oblivious to the danger, were still fighting over robes. Most just wanted to get out, and the crush of bodies heading for the door became a living thing that reached out and sucked my father into its mouth. I couldn't even see him now, and my shouts were lost in the general uproar.

I got another breath of smoke and started to cough. Panic seized me. The front door was too far away, the mob too thick. I spun off and headed for the nearest window, but it was jammed and wouldn't open. I grabbed half of a broken chair, smashed the window, climbed over the edge, and leaped out into the night.

Now what? The first thing I decided to do was ditch my robe, which was soaked with the blood of the woman my father had killed. I wanted it away from me.

Once I had stripped it off, I used it to wipe my hands, which were also covered with blood. Even though I got rid of the worst of it, they wouldn't come clean.

I wondered if they would ever feel clean again.

I shook myself. I didn't have time to worry about that. We needed help, and needed it bad.

Where, I thought wildly, *are the cops?*

I raced toward the gate, where the cops had been parked. The screams and shouts behind me were appalling. Surely the cops could hear them.

When I got to the gate, my heart sank. One of the cop cars had crashed right through it. The fencing was tangled under the tires.

What was going on here?

Figuring I could at least use their radio to signal for help, I wrenched open the car door.

I nearly sobbed in frustration.

The radio had been shot out.

What hadn't made sense before was suddenly clear. Somehow the LMCs had gotten the jump on the cops, then used their cruiser to break through the gate.

But what happened to the cops themselves?

I headed for the other cruiser, on the slim chance that it still had a working radio.

It didn't.

What it did have was four cops sprawled on its seats. Two were unconscious.

The other two looked dead.

I backed away from the car, reeling with horror. Why hadn't we heard this happening? How had the Angels missed it? Had they been too busy focusing on that final ceremony?

More pressing than any of those questions was this one: *What do I do now?*

Then I had it. My laptop! If the battery was still working, I could pull up the cell-phone function and use it to call for help. I cursed the fact that I had neglected to get the laptop back from Marina that afternoon—until I headed for her tent and saw that it was still standing, while ours had already been trashed.

I heard the crashing tinkle of windows breaking, and then more gunfire. Screams and shouts filled the air. I could smell the fire again, far from it as I was.

A shot zinged past, and I threw myself to the ground, terror racing through me like cold fire. I waited for another, then decided it must have been a stray bullet.

Even so, I crawled the rest of the way to Marina's tent.

Once inside, in the darkness, I started ripping through

it like a wild man, trying to find the laptop by feel. After a few seconds I found not the laptop but a flashlight. I had just flicked it on when Marina's mother showed up. Her robe was torn, her hair tangled, her face streaked with soot.

"You!" she shrieked, staring at me with wild eyes. "You hell-spawn devil-boy! What are you doing here? What have you done with my daughter?"

Then she lunged at me.

48

Marina

It was cold outside, and quiet after the heat and horror of the Great Hall. I could hear the fighting around front, and some sort of keening wail. But I had no desire to go and see what was happening.

Jillian and Ashlee and I led the line of white-robed children up to a small rise, with the noise of battle behind us. Grahame and Martin were at the rear.

"Shout at once if you hear anything coming!" I'd whispered to the boys. "You must be brave now. You have the hardest part of all."

"The *hero* part," Grahame said solemnly to Martin. And Martin, just as solemnly, nodded back.

There was not a single whimper, not a single complaint, from the little kids on that walk. The hysterical giggles had been swallowed up by the dark. They had no idea where their parents were. And having had the World's End drummed into them for well over a month, how could they not have been scared into silence?

I was scared myself. And I knew where we were going. Even when a pair of bats flew out of the trees and swooped overhead, except for Jillian's quick intake of breath, there wasn't a sound from any of them.

They were *all* heroes as far as I was concerned.

Once we got over the rise, I had them hold hands. It would have been horrible to lose one of them now, out here in the cold and the dark. I thanked God for their white robes, which let me keep track of them.

"If you get really scared," I said, "just touch the silver candle pin on your robe."

Obediently, they all raised their hands to their collars.

One little girl, the blond who'd been so scared in the Hall, raised her hand.

"Please, Marina," she said in a wispy voice, "I don't have my pin."

"You can have mine, Tanya," Jillian said. She handed the sleeping baby to me, took off her pin, and set it carefully in Tanya's collar. Then she reclaimed the infant.

"What will you do without yours?" Tanya asked.

"Big girls don't need pins," I said quickly, trying to forestall a theological debate. "We're Cherubs, after all. We get our courage straight from God. Our orders, too. Now be quiet. I'm going to count you all."

I counted out loud. "Fourteen!" I said. "Pick a buddy and keep track of your buddy carefully. Let Jillian or Ashlee or Grahame or me know if anyone gets lost."

"Me, too," said Martin.

"Or Martin, too," I said. I kept my voice strong. I didn't dare let them know I was frightened.

"Hup and one, hup and two," I called to them. "Like the soldiers in *Stone Soup*." I swung my arms and began to march.

241

They followed silently, a long white line.

After a second rise the noise of the fighting back at Cut House was only a babble behind us. By the next turning it was as if the attack had never happened.

I picked up the pace, and that meant I had to piggyback a three-year-old who was starting to lag behind. Since I was already carrying Leo, it made quite a heavy burden. But it was unthinkable that any of the children should get left on their own.

Grahame gave another little girl a ride on his back for a while, till he tired and had to set her down again. But she never made a sound of protest, just held tightly to Grahame's hand and went gamely on up the winding trail.

The rocky scree near the cave site was really tough going, slipping out from under our feet. Several of the children began to slide dangerously, and so I called a halt.

"I'll carry everyone across," I said. I tried to make it sound like a game, but my voice quavered a bit. I was so tired at that point, if anyone had objected I probably would have just collapsed on the edge of the scree and cried.

They all waited patiently while first I helped Jillian and the baby over the dark pebbly course, so she could keep an eye on the little ones when I went back for more. I left Ashlee, Grahame, and Martin till last. I didn't carry them, of course, simply led them by the hand across the scree.

The sound of those stones pattering down the steep mountainside away from us was terrifying. Yet the kids were so silent, we could hear an owl hooting nearby—a thin rise and fall of sound that was more like the sobs of a brokenhearted child than a bird.

When we got to the cave at last, I was the only one to

heave a sigh of relief. The others were not at all surprised at reaching it. I had promised them safety. And they were used to believing such promises.

"I'll keep watch outside," I told Jillian once we were all inside. "Just in case. You settle the kids down in here. Out of the wind, and snuggling next to one another, they should be warm enough. Those robes will make good pillows."

As I went back out I could hear her start to sing to them. She had a lovely, light voice, and sang with a kind of breathy eagerness.

She didn't sing hymns.

She sang "Dance to Your Daddy," "Lullaby and Good Night," and "Eensy-Weensy Spider."

After a while I stopped listening, staring out instead at the streetlights of one of the valley towns way below us, where the world had certainly not ended.

Only up here, on the mountain, had there been anything resembling Armageddon.

Made by man.

Not by God.

49

Jed

Mrs. Marlow beat at me in a kind of wild frenzy, as if she blamed me for everything that had happened, and under her fanatic attack I dropped the flashlight.

"Defiler!" she screamed. "Polluter! You never believed, never believed, and it soiled the mountain. This disaster is all because of you!"

I held my hands above my head, trying to fend off her blows. Finally I reached down with my right hand, grabbed the first thing I could find, and swung it at her.

I caught her in the side of the head.

She crumpled at my feet.

It was only then that I realized what I had grabbed, what I had hit her with.

It was the laptop.

She moaned, a low pitiful sound almost lost in the shrieks and gunfire filling the night air. I looked around desperately. I couldn't leave her here.

"Come on, Mrs. Marlow," I cried. "Get up. *Get up!* We've got to get out of here."

When she didn't answer, made no sound at all, I

dropped to my knees beside her, terrified that maybe I had killed her. Snatching up the flashlight, I pointed it at her. A trickle of blood rolled down her forehead. When I touched her temple I could feel a big lump.

Damn.

"Mrs. Marlow!" I screamed.

She moaned again, and I felt a surge of relief.

"Come on," I pleaded. "Get up. *Get up!*"

She didn't move.

I wasn't sure what to do. I needed to get into clear territory to make the call, and as soon as possible. And I needed to look for my father.

Yet I couldn't just leave her.

Still clutching the flashlight, I grabbed the laptop—and then one more thing that I noticed on the ground, which I tucked inside my shirt. Next I got my free hand around Mrs. Marlow's waist and dragged her to her feet. She didn't weigh all that much, and when I looked at her again I realized how much younger she was than my own mother.

I got her out of the tent. It was easy to see now, because of the brightness of the fire.

Feeling like I was going to explode, I moved as fast as I could along the line of tents, half dragging, half carrying her.

I hadn't gone twenty yards when I heard another woman sobbing.

Oh, geez. I can't stop, I thought. *I can't stop. Not now.*

I stopped.

It was Melinda. She was crouched in front of her tent, her head on her knees, wailing and beating her fists on the ground.

"What is it?" I asked.

"Agnes!" she cried. "I can't find Agnes! Jillian was holding her, and they've both disappeared!"

I hesitated for just a second. "Marina has her," I said, hoping desperately that I was telling the truth. "Marina took all the kids to a cave we know upmountain. I'm going there now with Mrs. Marlow. But she's hurt. Help me with her, and I'll show you the way."

She looked up at me, and in the light of the fire I could see hope in her eyes. "You're sure? You're sure Marina has my baby?"

"Positive," I lied—positive in any case that we weren't going to find the child down here, and that the best chance of saving both Melinda and Mrs. Marlow was to get them away from the mob. "Help me," I said again.

Melinda staggered to her feet and we got Mrs. Marlow centered between us. After that I was able to move a lot faster.

The path took us back toward Cut House, and I hesitated for a moment, wondering if we should go some other way, longer but safer, then decided against it because I didn't want us to have to be picking our way through the brush.

The building was really burning now, flames licking out all the windows. Men were shouting, racing around the edges of the light. Their words were lost in the roar of the fire, the sounds of the guns. I looked in vain for any sign of Dad. Had he made it out, or was he still inside?

Suddenly I saw L.A. coming out of the door, haloed in the fire. He was carrying a white-robed woman in his arms. I recognized her as one of the Lady Angels. Racing down the steps, he put her on the grass, then turned and plunged back into the burning building.

The gunfire continued, and I found myself praying that I would be able to get Melinda and Mrs. Marlow past this place without one of us getting hit by a bullet.

It was hard to tell who was shooting at who, since by this time most of the Believers had shed their robes. I wondered if the few who were still wearing them figured God was going to protect them from the bullets. As far as I was concerned, they might as well have been screaming, *Hey, look! I'm a target!*

Suddenly a voice sounded clear and strong even above the roar of the fire. It was Reverend Beelson. He was standing on the steps of Cut House, still wearing his robe, which was tattered and smoke stained. He had his Bible in his right hand, and both hands raised to the sky.

"My God, my God!" he cried in that huge voice. "Why have You forsaken us?"

One of the Angels—he had taken off his robe, but I recognized him—came racing out of the darkness. He grabbed Beelson's arm and tried to pull him down the Cut House steps to safety.

Beelson shook him off like an insect.

"My children!" Beelson roared. "All my children! Put down your guns! Come to my side! Pray with me! This is not the way we are to enter the New World!"

Could he possibly still believe in that demented vision of his? Even with the mountaintop version of Hell raging all around us?

I knew with absolute conviction that the only safety lay in moving on, getting away from the carnage.

But that scene held me riveted.

Melinda clutched my arm, whimpering but showing no signs that she wanted to move, either. Mrs. Marlow, who was barely on this side of consciousness, sagged by my side.

Another shot rang out.

Beelson didn't even flinch. "This is not the Way of the Lord!" he roared.

You should have realized that before you brought those guns up here, I thought. Yet at the same time I was awed by his courage.

Suddenly Beelson dropped to his knees. Still holding up both hands, he began to sing, his great baritone rolling out into the chaos:

> *Just as I am*
> *Without a prayer*
> *O Lamb of God,*
> *I come, I come.*

The fire crackled and raged behind him. I wondered how he could stay there. I figured his backside must be roasting.

But the gunfire stopped.

Men began to step out of the darkness, slowly, tentatively, joining in with Beelson's song.

For a long moment, it looked as if a miracle had occurred and Beelson had actually calmed the mob.

I took a deep breath and was about to start singing myself. But before I could get out the first word there was a sudden spray of gunfire, from an automatic weapon this time, and one of the sheds—the first one that I had helped build—exploded.

Some damn fool had hit a gas tank.

The ball of fire that rolled up from that little building was astonishing: Armageddon in full flower. Fire rained on us. Screams of horror erupted, and madness seized the camp again.

Beelson leaped to his feet and spread his arms, as if in appeal to the whole mob. Then his robe burst into flame. He stood, wailing a great cry of sorrow and loss as a halo of fire surrounded his head.

Mrs. Marlow began to scream.

A man raced out from the darkness. It was L.A. again, who must have come out one of the side windows. He hit his father with a running tackle, knocking him into the dirt ten feet from the door. Then he began rolling him over and over, until the flames were out.

I wanted to go over to them, to see if I could help. But what was there to do? Besides, Mrs. Marlow had fainted and was drooping against me.

The gunfire was still going on around us.

I shouted to Melinda. She turned to me, her eyes wide and horrified, and nodded.

We moved on, dragging Mrs. Marlow between us.

We had gone another thirty feet, maybe, when Hank stepped from behind a tree. He stood directly in front of us. His long, lean face was streaked with soot; one pant leg was torn open, revealing a jagged wound.

"Where you going, Jed?" he asked.

"Upmountain," I said.

He looked down at the laptop I had clutched in my right hand. "What's that?" His voice was tight, almost hungry, and I wondered if I was going to have to fight him, too.

"Laptop," I answered tersely, my stomach squeezing with fear.

249

"Got a cell-phone in it?"

I nodded, wondering what was going on.

"Good. Mine got fried, and I need to make a call."

Before I could say anything, he scooped Mrs. Marlow into his arms and snapped, "Let's get out of here, kid. I'll make that call as soon as we're in the clear."

He started forward, his stride strong and swift despite his wound.

I hurried to keep up with him, pulling Melinda along with me. It took about five minutes to get to an open spot where we could use the laptop's cell-phone, and by then Hank had convinced me it was safe to let him have the machine.

We sat on a broad expanse of rock, and while Armageddon raged below us, I pulled up the calling program.

I passed the laptop to Hank.

He tapped in a number. After three rings a female voice answered, "FBI, Special Sections."

"Annie, this is Agent Hummiston. I need help, and I need it fast. We've got fire on the mountain."

He talked for a little while longer, giving her some details. When he ended the call, he looked relieved. "They're on the way," he said. "Firefighters. Troops. Everything."

He stood up. "Take the women rest of the way up, Jed." He looked back toward the flaming hell below us. "I need to go back down there until help arrives. I'll see you up top later on. When it's all over."

I shook my head. "I have to go back down and look for my dad."

It was only in that moment that I realized Agent Hummiston knew what my father had done, knew he had killed that woman, even though he was only trying to protect me. Instantly my mind started spinning out wild ideas about finding Dad and leading him out through the woods, away from the mountain. We would go underground, change our identities, get away from this place.

Hank's voice snapped me back to the moment. "There's no point," he said softly.

At first I didn't know what he meant. He must have seen that, must have seen the confusion in my face, because he grabbed my shoulders, looked at me closely, and said. "There's no point in going down there to look for your dad, Jed. Do you understand me?"

I understood. I understood, too, that he didn't want me to force him to say it out loud.

I didn't want to hear it out loud.

I didn't cry. Not then. I don't know why. Maybe I had been scoured out by all the madness on the mountain. I just felt cold. Cold and empty.

I grabbed Hank's arm. "The only reason I came up here," I whispered savagely, "was to take care of him. I never believed any of this stuff. None of it!"

He nodded. "I figured," he said.

We stood that way for an instant, and I could feel myself vibrating. I was a heartbeat away from flinging myself against him, from breaking down and sobbing.

I didn't. I took a breath and turned away. "See you later. At the top of the mountain."

"At the top of the mountain," he repeated.

Then we turned and went our separate ways, Agent Hummiston back to the flames of Armageddon, me leading Melinda and Mrs. Marlow up the mountain, toward the stars.

251

50

Marina

I know what a real angel looks like.

Not a big man with a gun guarding an electric fence.

And not some kind of creature with wings that leak feathers like a down coat, either.

I was thinking all about angels as I sat on the mountain-top, guarding the entrance to our cave. I was cold inside and out. I was confused, exhausted, scared. I wondered what God was doing while we cowered there, so far from our parents. I wanted to pray but I didn't know the right words.

How about, "The Lord is my shepherd."

But *I* had been the one to shepherd the children through the chaos of Cut House. And the top of a mountain was sure no deep pasture.

It was awful being a hero at fourteen.

Even more horrible having to be the one in charge. Making life-and-death decisions. Like my mom and dad had to do before I was born.

No wonder Mom had been looking for so long for someone bigger to take charge.

Like Reverend Beelson.

Like God.

"O God," I whispered, "help me. I want to believe. I want to be comfortable in my belief again."

Behind me, in the cave, Jillian was still singing to all our frightened kids, and she wasn't all that unfrightened herself.

Every once in a while I could hear a little voice call out something like, "Sing it again, Jillian." Or, "I want my mama."

And I knew suddenly how much I wanted *my* mama, too. The one from downmountain. The one I had glimpsed for a moment in the hurly of the Great Hall.

I want... But I scolded myself, *That's magic thinking, Marina. Consider instead what's real.*

What was real was that we needed a guard. And I had been elected.

Well—I had volunteered, anyway.

I had to stay outside and keep watch.

We might have escaped the main violence at Cut House, but there was no guarantee more wouldn't come rushing up the mountain to find us.

I heard a noise at my back and someone came out of the cave to sit by me.

"Did you know..." he began.

I laughed, though it wasn't a really happy sound. "Don't know much, Grahame. But I've been thinking about angels."

"I've been thinking about Dad," he said. And then after a moment he added, "Do you think Dad knows?"

"About angels?"

"No, Marina. Do you think Dad knows where we are? Or what's been happening here?"

I thought a long time before answering. "He knows we're on the Cut."

"Then why isn't he up here with us?"

I took an even longer time answering that question. But I had to say something.

"Because," I said at last, "Dad was never a Believer."

Grahame turned to me, and I could read his face by the stars. "I was never a Believer, either, Marina. And I'm here."

It was time to be honest with him. And with myself. "You're here because Mom is here," I said. "And Dad is *not* here for the same reason."

He thought a long time about that. Longer than he needed.

"Is Mom dead?" he asked suddenly, his voice very quiet, not like Grahame's at all.

"Of course not," I said. But remembering the chaos and the gunshots, the flickering lights and the screams, I wasn't entirely sure.

"You don't *really* know ... not like I know facts." There was an accusation in his words.

Which was when I understood that Grahame needed to *know* things in order to feel safe.

"It's a different kind of knowing," I said. "Here..." I pointed to my chest. "And not here." I touched my head. I said it as if I meant it, and I hoped that would do—for now.

Grahame leaned against me and sighed, so I knew I had pulled it off.

I remembered a verse of Emily's then:

254

> *The difference between Despair*
> *And Fear—is like the One*
> *Between the instant of a Wreck—*
> *And when the Wreck has been—*

I had never really understood that poem before. I had just liked the way it sounded. But now, having been in the "instant of the Wreck," I knew—as Grahame knows things—just what Emily meant.

We sat there for a long time. We may even have dozed off. But suddenly there was a sound of pebbles sliding nearby, and we both sat straight up with a start.

Someone was coming gingerly across the scree.

"Get back in the cave," I whispered frantically to Grahame.

"I'm staying with you," he said.

"I'm older."

"I'm a boy."

"Grahame—"

"Please—"

So we stood and faced whoever was coming toward us on the top of the mountain. Together.

The sounds on the tumbling scree got closer, until we could finally make out three dark shapes approaching. Grahame slipped his hand in mine and it was like a piece of cold bread dough. Then suddenly he pulled away and began running toward the figures.

"Grahame!" I cried out. But his voice overrode mine.

"Mom!" he called. "Mom! You're alive! And who's that with you?" He started sliding on the rough scree, and someone dashed ahead and grabbed him by the arm, holding him up.

It was Jed.

"A kind of angel," Mom called back in a voice I almost didn't recognize, because it was so hoarse and harsh and exhausted and in pain. "Because he saved us. And see—now he's saved you as well."

Grahame got his balance and I could hear his indignant voice clearly. "*He* didn't. Marina saved us, Mom. And Martin and I helped. But did you know seventy-three percent of Americans believe in angels? With wings."

"Watch that sassy tongue of yours, Grahame Marlow," Mom said. "Not all angels have to have wings." They walked carefully across the last stretch of the scree.

"Not all heroes need halos, either, Mom," I said by way of greeting. "Especially not at the End of the World."

For a minute she didn't say anything. Then, "You seem different," she said. "Older."

"You don't," I said. "You seem like the old you again." I gave her my hand and helped her onto the solid rock.

"Did we do wrong in believing, Marina?" Mom asked suddenly.

"Never in believing, Mom," I said. "Just in what we believed."

I looked at Jed, haloed by starlight, and thought, *I believe in Jed, God. And I believe in me. That will have to do for now.*

Just then the third person asked pitifully, "Is my baby girl here?"

It was Mary. Whose real name, I soon learned, was Melinda.

"In the cave," I said. "She's safe. With the others." I turned to Jed. "An angel, eh?"

He shrugged. "It wasn't like that," he mumbled. "I don't think she remembers everything. Which is just as well." A strange look slid over his face. "Besides..." and his voice cracked the word in two. "Besides, if I was really some kind of angel, I'd have saved my dad."

"He's not...he's not..." I couldn't say the word, which was odd, since a week before I'd been anticipating the deaths of billions.

Jed looked at me sadly. "Armageddon," he said. "Dad believed it would happen. He wanted it to happen. And it did. For him. I couldn't stop it, Marina, though I tried. I really..." He took a deep breath. "I really tried."

He suddenly started crying silently, as if any sound would have made what happened even worse.

I put my arms around him and held him for a long moment, not feeling that awful thumping of my heart or the lurch in my stomach, just a sadness about the whole awful day.

At last he pulled away and said in a strangled voice, "Here." He held out something in his hand. I took it, wondering. It was a familiar small volume. I could just make out the title by the light of the stars. *The Poetry of Emily Dickinson.*

"Happy birthday," he said. "Happy twenty-seventh of July. Sorry I couldn't get you anything new. The store..." His voice cracked oddly. "The store was closed on account of a death in the family."

"Old is fine," I whispered. "Old is better. And you know how much I love Emily's poems." Inside, I felt a small prayer, *Thank you, God.* It wasn't much of a prayer, but it was a start.

Then Jed took my hand, and we sat close together on the rock outside the cave without speaking for so long—hours, it must have been—that the sky finally lightened in front of us and we watched as the sun rose up over the rim of our brand-new world.

FROM: emilygirl@aol.com
TO: hotjed@colnet.com
RE: What I Did This Summer
DATE: 9/18/2000

Jeddie:

The newspapers reported your dad's death.
Reverend Beelson's, too. And the others'.
They said there were twenty dead. And forty
wounded. My mom didn't want us to know about
it. "Bury the past," she said, meaning we
should forget it as if it hadn't happened.
She's that way with a lot of stuff in her
life. But when it gets UNburied—watch out!

Dad saved the newspaper clippings, though,
and Grahame and I got to read all about what
really happened. Or at least what happened in
the broader perspective, which is what my
journalism teacher says a reporter is supposed to write about. We kept the bad stuff
from Martin and Leo and the twins, of course.
They're really too young to know.

Did you get my card?

I've been thinking a lot about those two

259

weeks on the mountain. About the twenty
people who died. I had to write one of those
What-I-Did-Last-Summer essays and it all came
up in a rush again. You'd think that by now
teachers would be tired of the same-old-same-
old. I'm sure Mr. Woodson, the teacher who
asked for the essay, wasn't expecting what he
got from me. I mean, it was close to a hundred pages. That's probably why he wrote, "A+
Wow! You're some writer!" on it. Probably
thought it was fiction.

"Tell all the truth," Emily said, "but tell
it slant." Who in their right minds would
want to make this stuff up? I can attach it
as a file if you want to read it. But maybe,
having lived it, you'd rather not.

I'm not sure how I feel about being back in
regular school, but at least it gets me out
of the house. Though there are too many Zon-
dras and Tiffanis (with an i!) around, if you
ask me. Still, it's better than having Mom
teach us. Grahame, especially, is taking to
real science, though he's driving us crazy
just now as they're studying volcanoes. And
it's, "Did you know magma..." this, and "Did
you know tremors..." that, and using the word
spew in every other sentence. He built a
mountain out of plaster of paris that erupted
with a real kind of lava for his science
project. What a mess! They move on to

rainforests next week, and we're all looking
forward to the change.

Having to get a job means Mom is out of the
house, too, which is good, and not just out
to go to church. Church, by the way, is now
Bible Baptist Church in Northampton. Did you
know that the tattered man, Charlie, goes
there, too? He's got a nursing job at Mercy
Hospital in Springfield, in the geriatric
ward. He's really sweet on Mom, who seems
more grateful to him than loving. But maybe
with her it's the same.

I know last time I e-mailed you I said we
were going to Hope United Methodist in
Belchertown. But they were too quiet for Mom.
And don't get her started on the Unitarians.
We already tried them. "Where's God?" Mom
kept asking the minister. "Where's God in
this place?" I think they were glad when we
left.

The good thing about church, though, is that
afterward we kids get to go to Dad's for the
day. He and Rosellen have moved in together.
And she's pretty good about the six of us
showing up on Sunday. We are trying to get to
like her. She still has too many teeth.
(That's a joke.)

What's not a joke is this tricky question of
belief. Once upon a time it was really easy.

I knew what I believed in. Now I no longer have any such easy answers. I think my beliefs all got shed, like an old skin, up on the Cut. Nothing fits anymore. And I am still all raw and new and easily sunburned. The churches Mom takes us to don't seem to have the right shape or size or pattern of new skin or—am I getting too meddlefuric? I know that sort of thing bothers you. But I don't know any other way to explain it. Maybe I just have to let the new skin grow on me all by itself. Organically. You can tell me if you like my new skin when I see you at Christmas. And maybe then you can tell me what you believe.

Really.

That's a joke, too. Like Emily's "buying a smile—today." I am not very good at joking yet. Especially about my beliefs. But I am trying. Trying for you.

XXXXXX Marina

FROM: hotjed@colnet.com
TO: emilygirl@aol.com
RE: hey, babe!
DATE: 9/19/2000

Dear Marina,

I miss you. Miss you miss you miss you.

Other than that, Colorado's not bad. My mom
and her studboy photographer have a pretty
neat place on—get this—the top of a mountain. Well, not quite the top. But pretty
high up. And just plain pretty. Gorgeous,
actually. Mountains out here are a lot
bigger than they are back East. The air is
thinner. They call people in Massachusetts
Massholes.

Confession: Being up here gives me an occasional nightmare. Bad memories, you know? But
most of the time I like it fine.

I'd like it even better if you were here.

Hot news: I may be flying back East for Dad's
memorial service. I'm getting used to the
idea that he's gone, but it's not easy. I

didn't know how much he meant to me until he wasn't here anymore. Which is kind of stupid.

I haven't been very pleasant to live with, I'm afraid. I pretty much shut down for a while, shut everyone out. But I couldn't stay closed up. Not after the mountain.

Mom's been pretty good about putting up with it. Even when I punched a hole in the wall.

My sister, Alice, came to visit. That was good. I can talk to her. I wish she could have stayed.

Sometimes I go out at night, alone, and stare up at the stars. Sometimes, just sometimes, I get a hint of what I felt on the mountain that first night we met.

Sometimes I even get the feeling that I might be part of things again someday.

About Dad. I keep thinking that even if he had lived, who knows what might have happened with the law? I'm not saying it was all for the best. (That's one of the great stupid phrases of all time, imho.) I'm just saying— actually, I don't have the slightest idea what I'm saying.

I wouldn't tell this to anyone else, but the truth is, I've prayed about it—or whatever it is that I do. I know it's not what =you=

do when you pray. But it seems to help, some-how.

Which leads me to that question you said you were going to ask me at Christmas: What do I believe?

Wish I knew.

Oh, all right. I knew you wouldn't take that for an answer.

So here goes:

* I believe there's something bigger than us that we're a part of.
* I believe there's something inside us that you can't kill, that lives on afterward.
* I believe no one has a lock on the truth. Or the Truth, for that matter.
* I believe people spend too much time fuss-ing about details and not enough time look-ing at the big picture.
* I believe you have to connect, with people, with the world, to be really alive.
* I believe you are the best thing that ever happened to me.

XXOOXX

Jeddie [GAK! I hate being called Jeddie. Ex-cept when you do it. Does that tell you any-thing?]

P.S.: I'm attaching some files with a bunch of
stuff I wrote about what happened to us this
summer. I almost fell off my chair when you
said you had to write about your summer vaca-
tion. My litcomp teacher asked us to do the
same thing! I was kind of amused when I got
the assignment. "Baby," I thought, "have I
got a story for you!"

But really, Marina, it's for you.

Only you.